COWBOY'S FAKE GIRLFRIEND

J.P. COMEAU

Cover Design by Cover Couture

www.bookcovercouture.com

Bart

"I'm looking for a mind at work! I'm looking for a mind at work! I'm looking for a mind at work! *Whoa-oh-oh-oh-oh, whoa-oh-hooooo oh oh!*"

I danced around in my truck as I blazed a trail down the highway toward Conroe. If my brothers knew I'd become obsessed with that new musical everyone was talking about, I'd never hear the end of it. But dammit, if the songs on that soundtrack weren't catchy as hell.

"Now I've been reading *Common Sense* by Thomas Paine..."

I blabbed along to the words as I cranked up the music, allowing it to fill the cab of my truck. With my windows rolled down and the sun shining bright in a cloudless sky, it ushered me all the way back to my hometown. And it boasted of wonderful news to come. I needed to take the weekend and check back in on the business's new Remington office building project because we'd hit a lot of snags that had since been unkinked. Our new main office building would be closer to Will and Bryce's home base. However, it would get everyone off the ranch and separate our animal training from the petrol business, which would create a seamless transition into purchasing the refinery property.

My brothers were a bit wary of making this new place our business headquarters, especially given how much Bryce and Will loved Houston. But, with the decision to try to build the oil refinery plant here in Conroe to open up new jobs to the beloved people of our hometown, it didn't make any sense to have the headquarters an hour away. The only part of our business in Houston was our headquarters. And if we moved it to Conroe, then all of our business trips could be conducted right here in Conroe as well.

That meant more money influx to breathe life into this small town again, much-needed jobs for those out of work, and training opportunities and promotions and dreams being rebuilt.

I wanted to bring that to the people of Conroe.

After all, this place couldn't rely on the rodeos alone. That was seasonal, at best. And everyone seemed to struggle around the holidays before the warmer weather crept up on us again. Not with this refinery, though. If we could establish ourselves fully as a family oil company right out of our hometown, we could win over new and massive customers just with our down-home American-grown story. And with a line of people ready to interview for new jobs, it made us look even more successful than we already felt.

People ate that kind of shit up nowadays.

Still, I knew Bryce wasn't on board. For what reason, I had no idea. On paper, it seemed like the perfect plan for all of us. Bryce could run the company and still stay with his family. Will didn't have to keep traveling out of town for business now that he had a family of his own. And having the company move here gave me a reason to move home. I mean, someone had to look out for the business in Houston.

As I passed the sign ushering me into Conroe's city limits, I turned down my music. I breathed in the fresh scent of cut grass and cow manure as it filled me from my toes to my forehead. It always felt good to come home. And every time I came back, I was reminded of how much I missed it. I missed living in Conroe. I missed getting together regularly with my brothers. I missed the compound and spending my weekends horseback riding and exploring the untamed woods that surrounded our family's property.

If I could get both of my brothers on board for this kind of a change now that we were full steam ahead with the new headquarters, it would be a no-brainer for me to move home.

Which meant I would never have to admit to my brothers how much I missed them.

Which also meant I wouldn't get relentlessly teased for it until the day I died.

Suddenly, the air around me changed. Long gone was the

scent of fresh grass, and in its place was the scent of home-made fried chicken. My mouth watered as I pulled over onto the side of the road. I looked around, trying to figure out where the hell that heavenly smell was coming from.

And when I saw Pete's Chicken up at the corner, I made my way along the shoulder of the road until I pulled into the parking lot.

"Just what I need," I said with a smile that faded quickly with the bickering in the distance.

"Hey! I'm talkin' to you!"

"I said, leave me alone. That's all I want you to do."

"And I said I need to talk with you. You ain't duckin' me anymore. Got it?"

The growling voice set me on edge as I slammed out of my truck. I followed the sound of the yelling and arguing until both parties came into view. I didn't recognize the man, but I recognized her instantly. And when I saw a man with Luna pinned against her car, every ounce of me dripped with fury.

"I wanna know why the hell you keep shooting me to voicemail," the man said.

Luna's voice trembled with fear. "Because you wouldn't stop calling and texting. So, I blocked you."

The man gnashed his teeth. "You ever think about just picking up the fucking phone?"

She snickered. "And talk to someone I don't wish to speak with? No, thanks."

I watched the man knock her to-go order out of her hands, and I lunged at him. I wrapped my fist in his shirt and swung him around, placing myself between him and Luna. I heard her gasp as I brought the man close to my face, almost lifting him off his fucking feet. And it took everything inside of me not to whoop that man's ass right where I stood. "I believe the lady said she doesn't want to speak with you. So, I suggest you leave."

The man smiled at me. "All we were doin' was talkin'."

"Before you yelled at her, pinned her against her car, and knocked her food out of her hands?"

"Maybe she should pick up her phone, then."

I shoved the man away. "Or, maybe you should take the hint."

I felt Luna's trembling hand against my back, and I peered over my shoulder. "You okay, Luna?"

She nodded, but her tears told me a different story.

"You know her?" the man asked.

I turned my attention back to him. "Does that matter?"

The man chuckled. "Got your guard dogs on me now? You'd rather go through all of this than just pick up your fucking phone, El?"

I pointed in the man's face. "You got one last shot before I rid you of your teeth. Take it, or suck on milkshakes for the rest of your life."

And as the man shook his head, I watched him back up to a car that could only be described as a rusty tin can on wheels. But, once he made his way out of the parking lot and disappeared down the street, I turned to face Luna.

"What the hell was that?" I asked.

2

Luna

I couldn't think straight. It was even hard to see clearly. The only thing I seemed to be able to focus on was Bart and his voice.

His presence.

His scent...

"Luna."

I jumped. "Sorry. Sorry. I just—" I looked down at the spilled food all over my shoes, and I groaned. "I have to go back inside and reorder. Dad's starving."

Bart gripped my arm. "Wait, wait, wait, wait. Just give yourself a second to breathe."

I pulled away from him. "I don't need a second to breathe.

I need to get home. Dad's hungry, and this is all he wants right now."

His voice softened. "Luna..."

I slowly turned to face Bart. "I was here getting takeout for myself and my father because his new housekeeper-slash-cook has the day off. Why he gave her the day off after only four days on the job, I still don't know. But, I need to get this food home, and soon."

He gripped my shoulders. "After you take some breaths. With me, okay? In through the nose and out through the mouth."

As I breathed with Bart, I felt the trembling in my knees dissipate. My back grew stronger, and my head was rising higher as I held it upright. I rolled my shoulders back and popped my neck, getting rid of the last of the tension that had risen in my body. Then, I puffed out my cheeks with a sigh. "Thank you. I needed that."

He chuckled. "I could see that."

I groaned. "I really know how to pick the winners, don't I?"

He furrowed his brow. "Pick the winners? You mean—?"

I rolled my eyes. "Unfortunately, I went on a date with that guy. He's not very happy that I wasn't returning his phone calls."

"May I ask why you weren't?"

I scoffed. "He was just as aggressive with me on our date as he was then. And he didn't like the knee I placed right into his stomach."

I could've sworn I heard Bart growl. But, traffic was rushing by Pete's Chicken so quickly that I figured it was just a car engine buzzing on the road.

"How's your father doing, by the way?" he asked.

I drew in a deep breath. "Much better, now that he's mobile after his double-hip replacement. It's hell getting him to do his physical therapy, though."

He chuckled. "Old men will always be stubborn."

"Why is that, by the way? Is it some power struggle or something?"

He grinned. "Or something."

I giggled. "Anyway, I need to get back in and reorder food. But thank you. Honestly."

"Luna?"

"Yeah?"

"You sure you don't want to call the police or anything? I mean, how did he find were you were anyway after only one date?"

I shrugged. "I just ran into him here. I was coming out, and he was going in."

He paused. "You sure about that?"

I blinked. "Well, now, I'm not. Thanks for that."

"All I'm saying is that he seems pretty aggressive. If he was willing to push your boundaries on a first date and then act like this when he just 'runs into you,' who's to say he's done?"

"Seriously, Bart, you're freaking me out."

He held up his hands. "I'm not trying to."

"Look, the man was drunk and belligerent. He threw back

way too many drinks on our date, and he smelled slightly of alcohol when he cornered me against the car."

"I didn't smell anything."

I turned my back to him. "Look, I appreciate you looking out for me. Really. But, please don't make this a bigger deal than it is. I've already got enough on my plate."

"But, are you sure this guy isn't stalking you? Especially using his reasoning for just running into you?"

I paused on the sidewalk. "I really have to get inside."

"So, you won't mind if *I* call the cops just to tell them what I saw. You know, since I witnessed it."

I reached for the door. "Do whatever you're going to do. Men are good at that nowadays."

I ripped open the door and walked back inside before he could get another word in edgewise. What the hell was it with guys and their constant power struggles? I could take care of myself—always had, and I always would. My father raised me to be strong and independent. He always told me that if I could provide everything for myself, then all a man had to offer me was love and loyalty.

My father was a wise man.

Still, by the time I reordered and got it in my hands, there were three police officers outside speaking with Bart. I walked around them and got into my car, ready to take this piping-hot food back to my father's so I could calm the crankiness that was his entire demeanor every time his stomach growled the slightest bit.

Until a knock came against my window.

"Ma'am, I'd like to ask you a few questions."

I tried not to roll my eyes at the officer as I cranked my car and rolled my window down. "Yes, sir? Is everything all right?" I asked.

He thumbed over his shoulder. "Mr. Remington seems to think you were being accosted by a man when he drove up. You okay?"

"And like I told Mr. Remington, I'm fine. It's just a guy I went on a date with, and he didn't like the fact that I wouldn't pick up his phone calls. I blocked him, happened to run into him here picking up takeout, and he got upset because I admitted to blocking him. That's it."

The officer nodded. "Uh-huh. And he knocked your food out of your hand?"

"Yes, sir."

"Yelling at you?"

"More like raising his voice. He's a man, and they don't like it when they don't get their way."

He chuckled. "I've been married eleven years, ma'am. I never get my way, but that don't mean I raise my voice, as you so kindly put it."

I sighed. "Can I be honest for a second?"

"I'd like it if you were."

"My father is home alone with two barely mobile hips, and he's hungry. Very hungry. And if I don't get this meal home, he's going to attempt to get up and fix himself something, which is going to result in him falling and messing up his hips. Who's gonna pay for that surgery if that happens?"

He nodded. "Ma'am, I understand where you're coming from. But, we get called to a scene, we have to be thorough."

The more he questioned me, the more I felt the food growing cold in my lap. And by the time the three officers were done poking and prodding my mind for what had happened, not even the heat from my thighs kept the damn takeout warm. It burned me to my core. I was well over an hour late getting dinner back, and all because Bart had to stick his nose where it didn't belong.

What in the world is wrong with men?

"Is that your receipt?" Bart asked. His voice came out of nowhere before I saw his arm dip through my window.

"What the—hey! Give me that!"

He jogged toward the door to the restaurant. "Be right back, Luna!"

I groaned. "I hate this entire day."

The officer appeared at my window again. "Just need your signature here, here, and sign and initial here."

I did as the officers told me before I handed back their pen. Then, as they finally started clearing out, I watched Bart burst out of the restaurant. He held a fresh bag of takeout in his hands and two to-go drinks, and as he came up to my window, he stuck his arm back in.

"Two sweet teas, two large number sixes, one with coleslaw and fries and one with macaroni and cheese as well as mashed potatoes. No gravy, you're welcome for that. I also got you two a couple of cookies and a slice of cheesecake thrown in as well. Here, hand me that bag in your lap."

I shook my head. "Bart, you didn't have t—"

"Actually? Keep that bag and take this one. You can reheat food later. This stuff is great when reheated slowly in the oven—"

"Bart, why did you—?"

"And let me know how the cheesecake is. I've never had it, but it looks great. I got both the blueberry and the strawberry com—"

"Bart!"

He blinked. "What?"

I ripped the bag out of his hand. "I have to go. How much do I owe you?"

He stood up, shaking his head. "On the house. I hope you and your father enjoy it."

And as I stared up at him in annoyance, I watched the sun change the color of his eyes. Long gone where the dark-blue beauties I was used to staring up at, and in came charging that deep-sea green that made my heart stop in my chest. His smile lit up his entire face brighter than the sun reflecting in his eyes, and as quickly as he smiled, my anger and frustration faded away.

Part of me wondered if he'd ever ask me out, especially after we clicked so well at the Rocking R Ranch barbecue last year.

But, part of me was too hungry to stick around to find out.

3

Bart

"Stupid fucking men and their bullshit ego," I murmured. I flipped on my turn signal so hard the damn lever almost tore off. "Coming at Luna like that, he's lucky I didn't have my shotgun," I hissed. I swerved my truck onto Bryce's driveway. "Fucking pathetic piece of—"

The front door tore open, and Willow stepped out onto the porch. She waved me down as I drew in a deep breath, trying to calm myself as much as possible. The last thing I wanted was for my family to see how riled up I was. I didn't want them asking questions and poking and prodding because if they did, I knew I'd speak up. And I had a stark feeling Luna would call for my head on a stake if I talked about what had happened this afternoon. So, I put on my best smile as I hopped out of my truck.

"Willow. You look beautiful as ever," I said.

She giggled, her arms outstretched for me. "Teach Bryce a bit of that Southern charm, will ya?"

I jogged up the porch steps. "What? He's already letting the romance fall to the wayside?"

She embraced me. "Let's just say his idea of foreplay is a slap to the ass and unbuckling my bra with one hand."

I chuckled. "Sounds like romance to me."

She pushed me away from her playfully. "Men and their antics. No wonder some guys stay single for so long."

Bryce stepped out onto the porch. "And yet, here you are, Willow."

She smiled brightly. "Can't leave that good dick behind once you find it."

I snapped my fingers. "Told you; that's what keeps them around."

The three of us laughed and embraced before they ushered me into their home. And as I stepped into the foyer, a thought dawned on me. *I forgot to plan a time to follow up with Luna.* "Shit," I hissed.

Bryce patted my back. "Everything okay, man?"

I raked my hand through my hair. "Yeah, yeah. Just realized I forgot to do something before I left."

"Anything you need help with?"

I waved my hand in the air. "Nah, it'll be fine. I can place a call, if necessary."

Willow closed the front door. "The wild world of testing for another oil patch already missing you?"

I snickered. "It always misses me. Even when I'm there."

Bryce smiled. "So, what you're saying is you're useless."

I held out my arms. "All the more reason to move back home, provided I can secure a job."

Willow patted my shoulder. "This is where I go get drinks so you guys can talk shop. Set up anywhere you'd like. I'll come to find you. Bryce, you want your regular?"

He nodded. "Make that two. Bart loves the blackberry whiskey I buy."

"Oh, you got more Bird Dog? Someone must've taken a trip to San Antonio lately."

Willow made her way to the kitchen. "I'm sure he'll tell you about his visit with Uncle Ryan sooner rather than later!"

I blinked. "Uh, oh. That bad, huh?"

Bryce wrapped his arm around my shoulder. "Shit, you know how that man is. A brother to our father, but always acting like the biggest brother of them all."

I chuckled. "So, you were ready to slit his throat?"

Bryce held up his fingers. "I was this close, man. This fucking close."

I barked with laughter as he led me into their library. And not too far behind was Willow with two glasses, some ice, and that lovely blackberry whiskey already opened for us. I thanked her with a hug while Bryce poured the drinks. Then, she left us behind closed doors so we could talk.

And we really needed to talk.

"So," Bryce said as he handed me a drink, "have you stopped by the building yet?"

I shook my head. "Came straight here once I got into town. Well, that, and I picked up food. So, that kind of trumped things."

He sipped his drink. "It's going to be kind of an awkward setup. I mean, you're talking about establishing the headquarters for our petroleum company in the old bank building."

I sat in the chair behind me. "Have you ever been inside of that place, though? It's fucking massive. You see two stories, but there are two separate basements under that thing. That's a lot of square footage."

He sat beside me. "So, what are you thinking? Offices on the top floor, management and secretaries on the main floor?"

I nodded. "Then, that first basement can be an equal split between document storage and equipment storage.

"So, what's that bottom floor?"

I grinned. "The bottom floor is the best part."

"And why is that?"

I snickered. "Bryce, the bank's old vault is on that floor. A completely open space with more locked space behind this massive circular door. And, it's got a private elevator to get down to that floor that can be programmed only to be accessed by a keycard or a code."

He smiled. "Our meeting quarters. Very cool."

I pointed at my brother. "Exactly. It's a great space to entertain. We can put in a wet bar, coffee bar, get some chairs in there, make it cozy. It's got enough space to hold at least fifty people who can move and comfortably sit so that we can use the vault for more intimate meetings, and the rest of that space can be used for our bi-annual conferences."

Bryce clinked his glass against mine. "Dammit, Bart, this just might work."

Will's voice sounded in the hallway. "I'm pissed you're drinking without me, you know."

I smiled as I stood to my feet. "Get in here and give me a hug."

Will darted into the library and wrapped me up in a massive hug. We patted each other's back before Willow stuck her head in long enough to hand us an extra glass with a ball of ice. I poured Will three fingers while he pulled up a chair, settling in to discuss things I needed his approval on anyway. And when I sat back down, the three of us stared at one another.

"Can I just say that Dad would be very proud of us right now?" Will asked.

Bryce snickered. "That depends on whether Dad likes the idea of us moving the whole company to Conroe."

I shrugged. "He doesn't run this place anymore. We do."

Bryce held up his finger. "Yeah, sorry. *I* do."

I rolled my eyes. "You hold the position of CEO, but the three of us own this company equally."

Will nodded. "Yep. My stock portfolio says so."

Bryce chuckled. "At any rate, Will."

"Bryce."

"Have you been to that bank building we finally got the permits approved for?"

Will blinked. "Don't tell me you haven't. That place is amazing and full of history."

I held out my hand. "Right? Tell him, Will. He seems to think I'm selling him some empty plot of land with poison ivy all over it."

Bryce held up his hands. "It's not that I don't believe you. It's just that this is a very permanent move. We move and root ourselves here; then, there's no possibility of moving this to Houston. Which was the original plan, remember?"

I snickered. "Yeah, until you guys went out and had families."

Bryce turned to Will. "And speaking of, how are things going with Sadie?"

I followed his movements. "That's actually a really good question. How *are* things going with Sadie?"

Will smiled brighter than I'd ever seen in my life. "That's a completely different conversation, but let's just say things are out-of-this-world good right now."

Bryce wiggled his eyebrows. "Getting used to having the love of your life around, huh? Huh?"

But, Will's eyes fell to my knee. "You gonna stop jiggling that leg anytime soon?"

I quickly ceased its movement, but then my fingers started drumming on the arm of the chair.

"You good, Bart?" Bryce asked.

Will leaned back. "How long have you two been sipping on these drinks?"

I shrugged. "Only a few minutes. Why?"

Will nodded to my hand. "Because Bryce still has half of his, but yours is already gone."

Bryce's eyes flickered down my body. "What gives?"

Will grinned. "Yeah, Bart. What gives?"

I hated it when my brothers could read me like a damn book. But, I didn't want to invade Luna's privacy. Opening up to them meant talking about what had happened to her, and I didn't want to take that power away from her.

Will leaned forward. "Come on. If something's bothering you, then you need to get it out."

Bryce quirked an eyebrow. "Something happened while you were getting food, didn't it?"

I sighed. "Guys, look. I just—"

Will interjected. "Everything okay back home?"

Bryce scooted his chair closer. "You did say you needed to make a call. Is that what has you so anxious?"

I leaned back in my chair. "Can you guys just stop it for a minute?"

Will pointed at me. "There it is."

"There, *what* is?" I furrowed my brow.

Bryce nodded. "He's right. You always get defensive and need your space when something's bugging you."

I held up my hand. "You guys really need to stop. Okay?"

Will scoffed. "Oh, come on. It can't be that bad."

Bryce blinked. "Is it that bad?"

I rolled my eyes. "I just ran into Luna at Pete's Chicken, and she looked frazzled, that's all."

My brothers fell silent before Willow stuck her head into the library. "You said Luna looked frazzled? Why?"

I rolled my eyes. "Fucking great."

Bryce clicked his tongue. "Hey. Language. That's my girl you're talking to."

Willow waved her hand in the air. "He can shut the hell up. He doesn't hear the girls and me when we get together."

Will almost choked on his drink. "Wait, what do you guys do when you get together?"

Willow grinned. "Secrets."

I sighed. "I'm serious. It's nothing. Luna just seemed frazzled and went on a bit about her father. I'm just wondering how she's doing with her dad's recovery and all of that. She seemed kind of out of it."

Bryce got up to get himself another drink. "I'm not buying it."

Will shook his head. "Me, neither."

I looked over at Willow. "Maybe you could check up on her or something? She just seemed off when I ran into her."

She licked her lips. "I mean, I could do that later. But, the kids are giving me a run for my money. I'm sure she wouldn't mind if you swung by just to check up on her, though."

"I don't have her address. Really, it's okay. I'm sure she's fine."

I watched Willow whip out her phone before she typed something in. And before I knew it, I felt my phone vibrate against my hip. Will started cackling as Bryce walked back to his chair, and in the process, he exchanged my empty glass with another full glass of blackberry whiskey.

"Check up on her, Bart, if you're that concerned," Willow said. Then, she disappeared down the hallway.

"I'm surprised Sadie and Luna haven't killed her yet," Will said.

Bryce snickered. "She's conniving when she wants to be."

I blinked. "She sent me Luna's father's address, didn't she?"

Will and Bryce spoke together. "Yup."

I looked over at Bryce. "Shouldn't you probably do something about that?"

"About what?"

"Her conniving, as you called it."

He barked with laughter. "It's cute that you think I can control Willow."

Willow yelled from the kitchen, "Yeah! He can't control shit!"

I fell apart in laughter as Bryce held up his glass. He toasted his family and his health, to which Will and I did the same. And after throwing back my second glass of whiskey, I pulled out my phone, letting my eyes dance over the address in my text message inbox.

I turned over whether or not to do it, and when I should go by if that were something I wanted to do. I mean, would Luna be upset if I showed up? Would this get Willow in trouble? On the one hand, I didn't want to stir up anymore heartache for Luna. But, on the other hand, I wanted to check up on her. Make sure she was all right.

And make sure that bastard didn't come around again.

I'd love to see those golden eyes again, too.

Luna had the most unique look about her that made her as beautiful as ever. She had dark-brown hair that hung naturally down to her shoulders in soft beach waves that made me want to run my fingers through it. Her dark-brown eyes had golden flakes in them, making them almost seem like honey in the blazing summer sun. Her body was thick with curves, too. Sloping, luscious curves that made me want to pant like a fucking dog for a bone. But, the best thing about her was that she wore everything with pride. She never tried to cover herself up or pretend to be someone she wasn't. She wasn't into makeup or jewelry, and she didn't do the fashion thing. She was a very down-to-earth girl who also happened to be stunning.

She was perfect.

And that was enough to convince me to see her.

"Hey! Bart!" Bryce exclaimed.

Will waved his hand in front of my face. "Earth to Bartholomew. You there, dude?"

I blinked rapidly. "Don't you ever say my name like that again."

Will grinned. "Don't zone out on us like that, then."

Bryce patted my shoulder. "You good? We lost you there for a bit. You really that worried about Luna?"

Will chuckled. "Yeah, he wasn't worrying over her just then."

I glared at my brother. "You'd know, right?"

Before Will and I could face-off, Bryce got up and stood between us. I relaxed heavily into the wingback chair, allowing my drink to settle between my thigh and the arm of the chair. I closed my eyes and drew in deep breaths, trying to calm the rest of my anger that I didn't have an outlet for yet.

Then, Will's voice sounded in my ear. "You got somewhere to stay while you're in town?"

Bryce piped up. "Yeah, you're always welcome to stay here with Willow and me and the kids."

My eyes slowly opened. "As grateful as I am for your offer—"

Will snickered. "I didn't offer shit. I was going to offer Bryce's guesthouse."

"Thanks," Bryce said flatly.

I stood to my feet. "At any rate, I've already got a hotel room booked for myself while I'm overseeing things."

Bryce set his glass down. "And steer jerking. Don't forget that we have the training and practice hours while you're in town."

I smiled. "I don't ever forget my steer roping responsibilities. You know that."

"All right, all right. Just making sure Luna's big doe eyes hadn't compromised you, is all."

My face fell flat. "All right, I'm out of here."

Will started laughing. "Going to pay a visit to Miss Luna?"

I flipped him the bird. "Actually, I'm headed to the gym. Gotta work out some feelings."

Bryce called out after me, "Some sexual feelings!"

And as my brothers snickered with one another, I made my way for the front door, focusing my mind on the next two hours and everything I wanted to accomplish in the gym.

Then maybe, just maybe, I'd shower up and go knock on Luna's door. You know, just to make sure she and her father had everything they needed.

4

Luna

I placed my phone onto the counter while I stirred the spaghetti sauce. "I've got you girls on speaker. Dad's upstairs right now, showering and getting changed. I don't have a lot of time to talk, though. Everything okay?"

Willow was the first to speak up. "So, what's this I hear about you running into Bart this afternoon?"

I paused my stirring. "What?"

Sadie giggled. "You're so cute when you're caught off-guard. You know that?"

Dad yelled down the stairs, "El!"

"What?"

"Where the hell are my pants?"

I rolled my eyes. "In the second dresser drawer from the top on the left!"

"I always keep them on the right side. You know this!"

I shook my head. "Then, do your own laundry!"

Willow barked with laughter. "I love the relationship you have with your father."

I sighed. "That makes one of us some days."

Dad called out again. "El!"

I put down my stirring spoon. "If you wanna eat tonight, dress yourself!"

Sadie giggled. "You know he's doing all of this because he isn't ready for you to leave yet, right?"

I picked up the spoon. "Yeah, well, that makes two of us. As much as Daddy drives me nuts, I'm still worried about him."

Willow cleared her throat. "While I want to jump down this rabbit hole, I know you're using it to deflect from Bart. You ran into him. Why?"

I rubbed my neck. "Uh, the whole idea of running into someone is grounded in the fact that it wasn't planned. Ergo, no actual purpose."

"Then, why was Bart at my house all frazzled because he was magically 'worried' about you and your father."

I paused. "He said that?"

Sadie piped up, "Something happened, didn't it?"

I quickly picked up my phone and took them off the speaker. "What else did Bart say?"

Willow sighed. "Luna, if there's something—"

I hushed my voice. "What else did he say? It's important."

Sadie swallowed hard. "You're scaring me. Something happened. What happened, Luna?"

"Yeah," Willow said, "now you've got me worried."

I pinched the bridge of my nose. "Remember that guy from the gas station I got to talking with?"

Willow clicked her tongue. "That terrible first date you had?"

Sadie sighed. "You called us up crying after it. Of course, we remember. Why?"

I leaned against the kitchen counter. "I went to Pete's Chicken to pick up takeout and kind of had an altercation with him."

Willow scoffed. "I'm sorry, but what?"

Sadie hopped in, "What kind of altercation?"

"He didn't put his hands on you, did he?"

"I'm gonna kill that fucker if he—"

I shook my head. "He didn't put his hands on me, but there was yelling. He's pissed that I blocked him and wasn't picking up his phone calls, and in the process, he knocked the food I ordered out of my hands."

Willow gasped. "You're kidding."

Sadie's voice grew stern. "I hope you called the police on his sorry ass."

I closed my eyes. "Honestly? I just wanted to get out of there. Bart showed up right when he knocked the food out of my hand and got the guy to go away. Then, he's the one who called the police."

Willow snickered. "And let me guess, you didn't want them called."

"No. I didn't."

Sadie paused. "Wait. So, Bart kind of came to your rescue."

I scoffed. "I didn't need rescuing in the first place. I had it under control."

Willow giggled. "Says the waver in your voice. You were glad he showed up to help, don't even lie."

"Yeah, I saw you at that barbecue a little while back. The two of you were stuck together like glue."

I grinned. "I'm surprised you noticed with how far up Will's ass you were stuck already."

Dad's voice sounded behind me. "You know how I feel about that kind of language, El."

I jumped at his voice. "Sorry, Daddy."

"And that's our cue," Willow said.

Sadie started shuffling around. "Any last words before we part?"

I shook my head. "Nope, other than I love you, girls."

I heard Sadie's smile through the phone. "I love you, guys, too."

Willow sighed with relief. "I'm just glad you're okay. I love you, too. But, there's one more thing."

I took the noodles off the hot stove. "What is it?"

Willow talked quickly. "I kind of gave Bart your father's address so he could come to check on you. Love you. Bye!"

I blinked. "Wait, you did wha—"

The call dropped before I could even question what the hell she had just said, and I didn't know how to feel about it. Why in the world Willow always felt the need to stick her nose in things like this, I'd never figure out.

"Dinner ready yet?" Dad asked.

I drew in a deep breath. "By the time you make your drink and sit, we'll be good to go."

He harrumphed. "You got garlic bread to go with that spaghetti?"

"Staying warm in the oven."

"What about dessert?"

I rolled my eyes. "Cobbler's just gotta be reheated, and then there's vanilla and caramel-swirled ice cream. Just like you wanted."

"El?"

I spun around. "What?"

I found his eyes softer than usual. "You ever need my shotgun out of my truck, I don't care if you carry it around in your car."

My eyes watered. "I love you, too, Dad."

He hobbled over and patted my shoulder. "This stuff doesn't have to be in bowls and shit. Just get it on the table, and let's eat. And no crying. I fucking hate crying."

I wiped at my tears. "Language?"

He chuckled.

"I'll let it slide this time."

I tossed everything onto the table and pulled out some paper plates. My father put off a lot of people, but he and I were as close as close could get. Yeah, he was rough around the edges. Yeah, he was gruff and silent most of the time. And yeah, he expected a lot from people. But when he loved you? He did everything in his power to make sure you had what you needed and that you were happy.

No matter what it cost him.

The issue was that his taking care of others usually came to his detriment. That was one of the reasons why he struggled with his health now. My father had barely broken sixty years old, and here he was with a knee replaced, both of his hips now replaced, and a full set of dentures. He never took care of himself when someone else was in need around him, and I was watching him deteriorate slowly. He was developing heart issues, which I knew stemmed from his "manly man" sort of exterior.

He never cried, or let loose with laughter, or smiled, or enjoyed his happiness. He never talked about his issues long enough for anyone to be able to help him, and he always took the brunt of the blame for anything that happened. Anything to spare those around him. All his life, he had worked himself to the bone without any regard for how it made those around him feel. How it felt for all of us to watch him slowly waste away in his masculine antics.

Watching this shit with my father was one of the many reasons why I'd never dated much. That and at least a third of the men in Conroe were too scared of my father to come within ten feet of me anyway.

"So, how are you feeling?" I asked.

Dad twisted some noodles onto his fork. "Fine. You?"

I picked up a piece of garlic bread. "Fine."

"That's good."

I nodded. "Uh-huh."

He picked up his sweet tea. "How are the girls?"

I smiled. "They're good. They say 'hey.'"

"Tell 'em I said to stay out of trouble with those boys of theirs."

I giggled. "You mean, the fathers of their children? You know Sadie's about to burst any day now, right?"

"She had a good pregnancy?"

I shrugged. "Far as I can tell. I don't see them too much nowadays since they both have families. But, we do what we can."

That was the extent of the dinner conversation with my father. He wasn't much of a talker, and I didn't care for idle and mindless chit chat. But, after dinner was over and Dad retreated into the living room to turn on the news, my mind started wandering as I cleaned up the kitchen.

Specifically, I started turning over the idea of moving back into my apartment.

Dad had been gracious enough to pay my rent out of pocket, even though I'd been staying home for a while now to help him out. But, the mere idea of going back to that place and learning how to live alone again seemed daunting. I'd gotten used to waking up with someone else here. I had gotten used to having someone who would sit with me at night and watch television, or go with me to the grocery store, or try out my latest dessert concoction in the kitchen.

I'd miss him once I moved back. But, I was ready for my own space again.

"Hey! El!"

My father's voice ripped me from my trance. "What?"

"Someone's here!"

And that's when I heard a firm, steady rapping against the front door. I wiped off my hands. "I got it."

My father murmured to himself. "Who the hell bothers someone at dinner time? Go home and eat somethin', ya idiot."

I giggled. "For all you know, Dad, it's not dinner time for them yet."

"Well, it is for us."

I reached for the doorknob. "Technically, our dinner time ended fifteen minutes ago when you got up and came in here."

He waved his hand at me. "Sassy, like your mother."

I pulled the door open. "And you know you miss it."

Dad's face grew somber. "More than I care to admit."

My heart broke for him, but I put on my best smile and turned my eyes to the person on the other side of the door.

"Hey there. Can I help... you...?"

And when he stood on the porch smiling with his hands shoved into his pockets, my heart stopped in my chest.

Bart.

"Hey there, Luna," he said.

"Who the hell is that?" Dad asked.

My eyes traced his body as I tried to register what was happening. Right, right. Willow gave Bart my father's address. But, all of that just happened today? What was he already doing here?

"Luna!" Dad exclaimed.

Bart chuckled. "Just me, Mr. Faircloth."

Dad harrumphed. "Tell that Bart boy to get in here and quit letting the air out."

I knew that was a bad idea, though, so I ripped myself out of my trance. "I'm going to speak with him on the porch. I'll be back in a second to finish cleaning the kitchen," I said.

Dad clicked his tongue. "My shotgun's in the closet, El."

I shook my head. "Noted, Dad. Thanks."

As I stepped out onto the porch, the scent of oak and cherry overtook me. The smell was so rich and so decadent it almost made me moan as I closed the front door behind me. I let my eyes pan up Bart's body, rife with muscle and teeming with a tan. And when his dark-blue eyes came into view—accented by the honey-brown natural highlights in his chestnut hair—I finally felt my heart kickstart again.

Bart was easily the most handsome man I'd ever set my eyes on.

And I could've sworn he was studying me the way I studied him.

5

Bart

I silenced my sigh as I held the phone to my ear. "Artem, I'm fully aware of all of this. We've been over this a dozen times. The numbers haven't—no, you can't go by what the market's doing. Why? Because we haven't hit the market yet. That's like saying 'five out of ten restaurants that open up right now are going to fail because five out of ten restaurants on Main Street have shut down.' The argument makes no sense."

I pinched the bridge of my nose as I leaned against the wall. I was getting frustrated with these pristine and proper men from Houston who kept climbing up my ass and attempting to make a home for themselves. One day, we had a deal to get financial backing for this refinery from the investors in our parent's original petroleum company. The next day, we had someone calling us with reservations and issues and statistics on the market plummeting and updates on the latest oil leaks in the Gulf that had absolutely nothing to do with us.

It was draining, to say the least.

And while I usually had my brothers to pass some of this burden off to, both of them were busy with their families. Bryce was up to his ears in children and demands from Willow. Will was on Sadie's heels constantly for no other reason than the man was head-over-heels in love. Sure, I was happy for my brothers. In fact, part of me was even a bit envious of what they both had.

I needed help with this family business, though. And there was no family around to help me out. "I need an assistant," I murmured.

"What was that, Bart?" Artem asked.

I cleared my throat. "Nothing, sir. The only point I'm trying to get across is—"

"You're right."

I blinked. "I know I'm right. But, what just convinced you that I'm right?"

He chuckled. "Your confidence, Bart. You have all of the persuasion your father always had."

I grinned. "Thank you for the compliment."

"Trust me; it's not always a compliment. But, at any rate, I'll contribute what you're asking under one condition."

"Name it. You've always been loyal to our family, so whatever makes you comfortable—"

"Find a balance."

I paused. "Come again?"

"Find a balance in all of this, Bart. Like your brothers have."

I shook my head. "I'm not following."

"You're a workaholic, that's what I'm saying. Your brothers, too. But, they've found their happiness outside of work. I want that for you, too."

I chuckled. "You don't have to worry about that, Artem. I promise I don't need a woman to—"

"I'm not talking about a woman or a family. I'm simply talking about whatever makes you happy. And not that rodeo shit, either. Your mother always had heart attacks when the weekends came around over it."

I blinked. "She did?"

He cleared his throat. "Find something outside of all this that makes all of this worth it. Promise me."

I nodded. "You have my word, Artem."

"Good. Now, get to work."

"Kind of ironic considering the conversation, don't you think?"

"Don't push it, Bart."

"Yes, sir. I'll get to work. And thank you for the show of faith."

As I hung up the phone, my mind came back to the knee-jerk reaction I had moments ago. An assistant. It honestly wasn't a bad idea. Bryce was leaning on Willow to help him with some of the stuff he had going on with work. She had become somewhat of a secretary to him, and I knew Will went home frequently and got Sadie's advice on things going on in the office. So, what was preventing me from hiring someone to help me out? I had the money to do so. I just needed to find someone with managerial experience.

Luna has that.

I shook my head and walked over to my laptop that was sitting next to my hotel-suite window. I picked it up and threw open the balcony doors before flopping down onto one of the lounge chairs afforded to me. Just because I wanted to see someone more often didn't mean I had to hire them for this position. In fact, hiring Luna could be dangerous because I might not focus with her around whether she had experience in the area or not.

"Luna, you look lovely this afternoon."

She looked up at me with her beautiful doe eyes and smiled. "Bart! I didn't know you were in town for the barbecue. How are you?" She got up and hugged me tightly, despite the grimace on her father's face.

"Bart," he said with a curt nod.

I released Luna. "Mr. Faircloth. How are you feeling?"

He shrugged. "Like shit."

Luna hissed. "Daddy."

He picked up his water. "What? It's the truth. Why lie to the boy?"

I chuckled. "It's okay, really. It's better that he's honest. Can I get you anything, sir?"

He pointed. "Sit."

I sat down next to Luna and watched him eye me carefully.

"You look good," he said.

I nodded. "So do you, for a double-hip replacement."

Luna put her hand on my forearm. "Please, tell my father that quitting my job was necessary to take care of him. Maybe he'll listen to you."

I peered down at her. "You quit your job? Why not just hire him some in-home care?"

Her father grunted. "That's what I said."

Luna clicked her tongue. "Daddy, I wasn't going anywhere with that grocery store anyway. They've refused my request for a promotion from management to upper management for months now. This is better for all of us. I get more time with you, and you have someone taking care of you that you trust..."

But, her father only rolled his eyes before taking another long swig of his water.

"Wish it were beer," he murmured.

Luna's face fell flat. "It fucks with your medication, Dad."

My eyebrows rose. "She's probably got a point there."

Her father whipped his eyes up to her. "Don't you dare curse at me. I didn't ask for any of this."

Luna snickered. "Says the man who would call me three times a day to help him out of his recliner because his hips hurt too much to get up on his own."

I pulled myself out of the memory of the barbecue and focused on what I was doing. As I scrolled through employment websites, looking for a possible assistant, I couldn't stop the nagging sensation in the back of my mind. Luna had years of managerial experience. And she was efficient. If she could take care of the work I had for her with half the zeal with which she did everything else in her life, this refinery would be up and going before the end of the year.

"Dammit," I murmured.

I shut my laptop and decided to run a few errands. I still wasn't convinced that offering Luna the position was a good idea, so maybe a bit of running around would help. I needed a few more groceries for the small hotel suite kitchen as well as another bottle of shampoo. And, I was craving a nice, chilled bottle of red wine. Maybe with a dry bite to it.

It didn't matter that I needed to clear my head, though. It didn't matter that I needed groceries. It didn't even matter that I'd only just run into Luna that afternoon at Pete's Chicken. I needed to see her. I needed to check in on her.

I needed to make sure she was all right.

So, before I knew it, we were standing on her porch after dinner time, with the moon hanging high in the sky and the stars twinkling in those gorgeous eyes I couldn't get out of my dreams.

"So," Luna said as she closed the door behind her, "Willow told me she gave you my father's address."

I nodded. "She did, yes."

She giggled. "Guess my best friend's at it again."

I furrowed my brow. "I'm not following."

She waved her hand in the air. "Not important. Is everything okay?"

I slid my hands into my pockets. "I just wanted to make

sure you were all right from this afternoon. You know, after that guy approached you and all."

"And you called the police even though I told you explicitly not to?"

"Would you have done the same if you were in my shoes?"

She smirked. "I'm pretty sure you can hold your own against a guy like that. So, give me the benefit of the doubt next time."

I chuckled. "Noted."

She licked her lips, and the motion pulled my eyes to that pouty lower lip of hers. Some days, I wondered what it might taste like against my own. Was it soft? Lightly chapped? Did she wear lip gloss or flavored Chapstick?

"Bart?" she asked.

I blinked. "Yes?"

"Did you hear me?"

I sighed. "I'm so sorry; it's been a whirlwind of a day."

"You and me both."

"Right, right."

She cocked her head. "There something on your mind; you want to talk about it?"

Want to come work with me so I can stare into your eyes all day? "Just checking up on you. Making sure you're okay and don't need anything. I'm on my way out to run some errands—groceries and stuff like that. You guys need anything?"

"Actually, if you're running out, we could use some more tea packets. I made up the last batch of sweet tea, and I haven't gone out to get more tea packs yet."

I nodded. "What brand do you use?"

"Usually, Lipton. But, if Nestea is all they've got on the shelves, I know how to doctor it up."

I grinned. "A Lipton lady. I like it."

"Is there any other kind to make?"

I kept coming back to her eyes. The smile behind them and the way they made me feel as if I were walking on air. Every time Luna looked at me, my knees trembled. Every time her body heat washed over me, it made my heart stop in my chest. She was a gorgeous woman, but more than that, she was kind and caring. She had a big heart and a lot of love to give, and she was devoted to her family.

I admired that greatly about her.

In any other world, she would've already been mine. But, her father was a petrifying man. I'd heard the stories from my friends around me growing up of all the intimidation tactics he used to keep boys away from Luna when we were all in school. And the horror stories were enough for any young man to keep his hands in check and his dick in his pants. And I wasn't even on the receiving end of his shit.

"Bart!"

I jumped. "Sorry, sorry."

Luna sighed. "Just spit it out. There's obviously something you want to talk about, and honestly, I could use a bit of a distraction."

I leaned against the porch railing. "Why's that? Is something the matter?"

She giggled. "One issue at a time, yeah? What are you thinking about?"

Might as well at least ask. The worst she can say is no.

I drew in a deep breath. "Well, my job is pretty much getting to the point where I need some help."

"Are your brothers not helping?"

"I mean, they're pretty occupied with their families. And I'm happy for them, but it dumps a lot of work on me. I was on the internet before I came over here, scouring resumes for someone who might make a good assistant."

"But you didn't find anyone yet?"

I shrugged. "I need someone with managerial experience and flexible hours. Someone I can call at the drop of a hat to meet me somewhere, even if it's at nine at night."

Her eyebrows rose. "Wow. That's a pretty hefty demand."

I nodded. "It comes with a hefty paycheck for a reason."

"Benefits of any kind?"

"The standard. Health insurance provided by the company. 401(k), if they were interested in something like that."

"What about vacation days?"

I folded my arms across my chest. "Usually, we start with twenty workdays of paid vacation and seven workdays of half-pay medical leave for any reason, but I'd be willing to negotiate that for the right person. I just have to find them."

Luna nodded her head slowly. "Is the position permanent? Or temporary?"

I raked my hand through my hair. "Honestly? I don't

know. Temporary, for now, I think. But, once the refinery gets up and working and I move back to help run it, I'd probably hire my assistant on full-time. I don't want to take Bryce and Will away from their families, but I need someone I'd be able to rely on during the workdays."

"I see, I see."

I searched her face. "What are you thinking?"

Then, she smiled at me. "I think I might want to put in an application under the assumption that the job can't be permanent for me. It'll only be a temporary thing."

My eyes locked with hers. "Why's that?"

She shrugged. "I don't think my dream is to be someone's assistant for the rest of my life. But, it does sound like a fantastic opportunity, and Dad's been bugging me to get out of his house and leave him alone for a while."

"Have you moved back into your apartment yet?"

She sighed. "I'm about to. Dad's doing well with his physical therapy and doesn't need me for much, other than food and cleaning. I can come by once a week and knock out all of that stuff, do some freezer meals. Things of that nature."

"If I offer you the position, will you tell me the other reason why it's only temporary for you?"

She gasped playfully. "Why, Bart? You mean to tell me I don't already have the job?"

I chuckled. "Cute. But, I know you're not telling me everything there is."

"And as someone in need of someone else, you're not really in a position to make a demand like that."

Touché. "All right. Here's my offer: a full-time position, six hours a day. Four of them will be with me, two of them will simply be you on-call should anything arise. Monday through Saturday, Sundays off. No evening work unless it's an emergency, and even then, any overtime you accrue is time and a half."

She chewed on her lower lip. "I like it so far, go on."

I smiled. "Twenty paid days of vacation you can cash in, seven half-pay days for a medical leave of any sort—and I can extend that to medical leave regarding your father at my behest—and the best medical coverage our company can offer."

"Do I get a 401(k) option?"

"If you want it, yes. The company offers matching deposits into a 401(k) up to six percent of the employee's paycheck, every paycheck."

"Will I have an office?"

I paused. "I can scrounge one up if you want. But, right now? I don't even have an office other than the balcony of the hotel room I'm staying in. However, I could probably set you up something at the ranch, if you don't like working from home or on your porch or anything like that."

"Do you have a pen with you?"

I thumbed over my shoulder. "Got one in my car. Why?"

"Get it for me. I need it."

I wasn't sure what she needed it for, but I trotted to my truck anyway. I came back with the blue ball-point pen, and she uncapped it before reaching for my wrist. She put the pen to my forearm and started writing something, but her hair was covering her writing so I couldn't see what she was doing.

"You're going to need to update your records in order to get me all of this hiring paperwork," Luna said.

And when she looked up at me and smiled, I realized what she had written on my forearm—her name, her number, and her apartment address.

Bingo.

6

Luna

I couldn't get my conversation last night with Bart off my mind. By the time I got back inside, Dad had already hobbled his stubborn ass upstairs. Which was odd, considering I figured he'd be peeking through a window to make sure Bart and I were at least three feet apart at all times. Nevertheless, whenever my father took his pain medication, it practically knocked him on his ass.

So, when I entered into a dark and empty house after Bart had left, it wasn't too much of a shock.

Still, I tossed and turned all night. I kept thinking about how wonderful Bart looked in the moonlight and how his clothes seemed to fit him just right. His T-shirt hugged the muscular indentation between his tricep and his bicep, which made it hard to focus on his beautiful face. Even out of the corner of my eye, I saw how strong his legs were. The rippling of his abs beneath his shirt called to my fingertips, and it almost tripped me up in the middle of our conversation.

And all night, I dreamt of the man beneath those fabrics.

"Luna!" Dad exclaimed.

I peeked my head out of the bathroom. "Dad! You okay!?"

"Your damned phone is ringing off the hook. Can ya pick it up?"

I blinked. "Sorry, Dad! I got it!"

With a towel wrapped around my body, I rushed down the hallway. I charged into my room and picked up my phone, silencing the ringer as quickly as I could. Great. Dad was already in a peachy mood for the day. That didn't bode well for the rest of the hours of today.

"Hello?" I asked.

Bart's voice sounded in my ear. "In the future, it would be nice if you picked up the first time I called."

"Well, in the future, I'm going to be up and going by a certain time so that I can wait for you every second of my day. But, right now? I'm working on my own time since I technically haven't onboarded yet."

He chuckled. "Which is why I'm calling. Can you zip by the hotel and sign this paperwork? It'll be quicker to process if you just come here and fill it out. There's a little cafe in the hotel I'm staying in, so we could grab a bite to eat, and I can help you through the paperwork. It gets pretty overwhelming for some."

I propped my phone against my shoulder. "If I were worried about being intimidated, I wouldn't be accepting this type of position."

"You have a great point there."

I smiled. "Keep complimenting me like that and I might just stick around."

"Trust me, that's one of my goals you're not supposed to know about."

My heart skipped a beat. "Anyway, go ahead and text me the hotel where you're staying. I'll get dressed and buzz by say, within the hour?"

"Sounds good. See you then."

"Oh, and if there's a cafe, does that mean there's room service?"

He chuckled. "Already wanting to enjoy the finer things?"

"Actually, no. My father's still healing, so the more people I can be away from, the more it lessens my chances of getting sick. His immune system is shot right now, so I'd actually feel more comfortable being away from people, if that's all right."

He paused. "I hadn't thought of that. Yes, we can do room service. I'll have a menu when you get here."

"I appreciate that, thank you. See you in a few."

"See you then."

I hung up my phone and quickly got dressed, then made my way downstairs. I heard Dad cursing to himself and grunting as he fought through his physical therapy exercises, and it gave me pause. I watched at the bottom of the stairs as he used the resistance bands to bicycle his legs. And despite the sweat dripping down his forehead, not once was he deterred.

You've got this, Dad. "Hey, Daddy?"

He sighed. "What?"

"I'm heading out for a couple of hours. Do you need anything while I'm gone?"

He groaned. "Arsenic that I can swallow."

My face fell. "Dad."

"Sorry. Sorry. Uh, nah. I'm good. Where you off to?"

"To fill out paperwork for a new job, actually."

His head slowly turned toward me. "A new job?"

I held my hand up. "Don't worry. It's only going to take me away four hours at a time. Four hours a day tops. The rest of it can be done from here, if necessary."

"No, no, no. I'm actually proud of you."

I blinked. "What?"

He put his feet back against the resistance bands. "Yeah. I'm proud of you. I was hoping you wouldn't go back to that awful grocery store you insisted on working at."

"Right. Well, I shouldn't be gone more than a couple of hours. Please, keep your phone by you and call me if you need anything."

He grunted as he stretched his legs out. "Will do. Bye."

I snickered. "Bye, Dad."

I walked out the door and punched in the name of the hotel Bart texted me into my GPS. It wasn't too far from me. A fifteen-minute drive, assuming no traffic. But, when I pulled into the parking garage and made my way inside, my jaw dropped at the sight. The place was luxurious.

"My word," I whispered.

I walked over to the elevator and slipped inside. I punched the number of the floor Bart was on and made my way to his room. And when he swung open the door, the smell of cinnamon and apples wafted up my nostrils.

My favorite scent.

"Come on in. I've got menus, the paperwork, and my laptop ready to scan it over to our HR Department."

He ushered me into the most fantastic hotel room I'd ever seen, and I couldn't stop looking around. The vaulted ceilings boasted of reclaimed wooden beams against a white backdrop that made the space feel bigger and brighter than most rooms. There was a small kitchenette that looked stocked with snacks and other things, and the French double doors leading to a private balcony were open, letting the breeze and fresh air filter into the room. The king-sized four-poster bed had sheer white curtains dangling down from it, wafting with the breeze as I drew in another deep breath of that wonderful scent.

Then, it hit me, and I turned to face Bart. "Why aren't you staying in your own place in Conroe?"

He closed the door. "Because I sold my place when I moved to Houston to take a job with the company I currently work for."

"So, what if this refinery or whatever brings you back? Where will you go?"

He turned to face me. "I'm looking for a place. But that always takes time. Finding the right house is paramount to me, especially since I do a lot of my work from home."

"Ah, you need a Zen sort of space."

He chuckled. "Something like that."

We stared at one another for a few seconds before he cleared his throat.

"I have the paperwork over here. Do you want to order food, and then we can get started?" Bart asked.

I blinked. "Yes, I'd love that. Where did you say the menus were?"

He pointed. "Right over there on the little breakfast nook."

I smiled. "I've always loved a little breakfast nook. They're so cute and intimate. Perfect for first waking up."

He led me over to the nook, and when we sat down, I felt his feet entangled with mine. Yes, breakfast nooks were intimate. But, they were also close quarters. I tried to focus as Bart guided me through the paperwork, from onboarding stuff from the company all the way down to the multiple signatures they needed for my medical benefits. But, before we hopped over to the 401(k) stuff, his worried voice caught my ear.

"Luna?"

I slowly looked up at him. "Everything okay?"

"I just realized we never really talked about the hourly pay this would be."

I shrugged. "I mean, I've got no issues with twenty-two dollars an hour."

"If I gave you twenty-five, would you sign on to working with me for the next three years?"

I blinked. "Bart, we've already agreed on this."

"I know, I know. You only want this to be temporary. But, if the pay is a problem—"

"It's not."

He leaned forward. "I'll give you a week's more of vacation time."

"That's not necessary."

"Another week of medical leave."

"Bart, that's not—"

He locked his eyes with me. "I'll double your paid vacation time."

I blinked. "Why are you so adamant about this?"

"Why are you?"

It hurt to even think about the answer to his question. There were so many reasons why I wanted—no, needed—this position to be temporary. And part of that reason was the fact that I was lonely. My two best friends had gone off and fallen in love with the Remington brothers, and I didn't want to start using my now-boss to fill that void. Just the idea of it reeked of disaster, and I didn't want any of that drama in my life. I'd gotten this far without the drama of a long-term man in it, and I didn't need to start muddying the waters now.

All I wanted was for things to settle down so I could move back to my apartment, get Dad back on his regular schedule, and start living my life the way I wanted to live it, without being around one of the reasons why I no longer saw my best friends.

Bart sighed. "On this next page, you'll need to specify a start date."

Thank you. "How about next Monday?"

He leaned back in his chair. "How about tomorrow?"

"Tomorrow's Sunday. That's when we're off, remember?"

He shrugged. "All right, so Monday."

"Next Monday."

"I'm going to need your services sooner than that. What about Tuesday?"

I smirked. "Thursday and I'm willing to work next Sunday if you need me to."

He chuckled. "Got some hot plans for the beginning of the week?"

"Just moving into my apartment. I'm going to need the time to get my things back and get settled in before I start this job."

"Do you need any help? I could provide my truck to chuck things in."

I giggled. "Agree to Thursday, and I'll take you up on that offer."

"I'll agree to all of those terms if you agree to one more thing."

I placed my pen against the last dotted line I needed to sign. "What is it?"

He smiled. "Come out with me tonight to celebrate. My

treat. Every new hire is celebrated in this company, and you'll be no different."

I paused. "Like, a party? Or, like dinner?"

"Probably more like dinner. I'll extend an invitation to my brothers as well as Willow and Sadie, but they've all been pretty busy lately."

I sighed. "Tell me about it."

I felt him studying me. "A dinner celebration wherever you want to eat."

My glance found his stare. "Wherever I want to eat?"

"Yep."

"Even if it's just fast food."

His face fell. "Luna. Come on."

I giggled. "I'm just kidding. I'm just kidding. But, seriously, there's this new seafood place that opened up downtown, and I've been dying to try it."

He pointed with his finger. "Then, sign and date one more time, and I'll call to make reservations."

And as I signed my name one last time, a little voice in the back of my mind reminded me not to get too wrapped up, not to lose myself in all of this. Just because I was lonely didn't mean that feeling needed to be at the wheel of this car that I was trying to navigate back onto the road.

Deep breaths, Luna, it's not a date.

But deep down, the wishful part of me wondered if it could have been had my life not taken so many drastic turns over the past few years.

❧ 7 ❧

Bart

I whistled to myself as I parked my car in front of the first piece of property Luna and I would see together on her first day of work. Even though the first week was usually set aside for onboarding and setting things up, I didn't see the purpose of that with her because she didn't have an officially designated office. So, with two coffees in hand and my book of notes crooked against my armpit, I stepped out of my car to wait for her.

"You're late," Luna said.

I whipped around. "Actually, I believe you're early."

She smiled. "Early is on time, and on time is late."

I handed her the mocha cappuccino I picked up for her. "One of those, huh?"

She plucked the coffee from my hand. "Thank you! And, yes. I'm most definitely one of those."

I smiled. "Good to know."

She took a long pull. "Oh, that's good. All right, what's on the docket for today?"

I set my notes in the bed of my truck. "Before the realtor gets here, let me see your phone."

"My phone? Why?"

I held out my hand. "I'm going to sync our calendars together."

"But, my calendar feeds into the one on my laptop."

I grinned. "Even better. That's how we can communicate our schedules to one another. I can add and detract meetings and appointments as necessary, and it'll automatically update, and you can put in things like your vacation days and days you need off for your father or whatever. Then it will automatically propagate on my end without us having to call and shoot emails back and forth constantly."

"That's... convenient."

Luna pulled her phone out of her purse and laid it on my palm. And together, we entered all of the information we needed to sync our calendars. We could deal with the idea of her work laptop at a later date because today was devoted specifically to seeing all of the properties that were available for us to purchase.

And hopefully, one of them was the magical one we needed for this refinery.

I handed back her phone. "Okay. So, today we're going to

see six different properties. They are the only six in the Conroe area that all have what we would need to get the refinery up and going, so hopefully, one of these six will work."

Luna slid her phone back into her purse. "And if they don't work? Are there any backup sites we're going to see that might take a bit more work, but could also be formatted to what the company needs?"

This is going to be perfect. "I'll have the realtor work on it if these don't work out."

Mr. Derecho sounded behind me. "But, I have a feeling one of these six will work."

I smiled as I turned around. "Mr. Derecho! Let me introduce you to my assistant, Luna Faircloth."

He held out his hand. "A pleasure to meet you."

Luna shook his hand. "Likewise. I have a question about this property already, though."

My realtor grinned. "She gets right to work, huh?"

I shrugged. "It's why I hired her."

Luna ignored our comments. "I can already see that a great deal of electrical work is going to have to be done. There are three main power lines down and disconnected, and the meters along the perimeter of the building are essentially rusted through. Any way that we can work out a deal with whoever owns this property to fix all of that up before we made a decision on the purchase?"

Mr. Derecho looked at me, and I stood by what Luna was asking. "I'd be interested in knowing that as well."

The realtor sighed. "Well, with the bulk of these proper-ties, the bank owns them. So, they're essentially sold 'as is.' But, they come at a heftily-reduced price. Take this property, for instance. It sits on seven acres of land, already zoned for business, and comes with the licenses necessary to expand if that's something you're looking to do."

Luna jotted down notes. "The price?"

"Two million."

My eyebrows rose. "That's it?"

He smiled. "That's it."

Luna didn't seem phased, though. "Any room for negotia-tion on that price?"

My realtor chuckled. "Let's take a look at the inside before we get into those questions, yes? Follow me."

As we walked through the first property, all eyes were on Luna. She asked some great questions, like the kind of piping for water that ran throughout the facility and the condition of possible office spaces, if there were any. She scribbled notes furiously in a binder full of paper she was carrying, and I felt my chest swelling with pride as we traveled from property to property. This woman was giving my realtor a serious run for his money.

"Miss Faircloth, I can assure you—"

She shook her head. "With all due respect, Mr. Derecho, I don't want assurances. I want paperwork. Unless you're willing to sign off officially on the statements you're making about these warehouses."

I leaned down to her ear. "If you want to impress me, you've already done it."

She cast a look up to me. "If you're going to get the best deal, you want to know exactly what you're walking into. Surprise work on a scale like this isn't ever going to be good."

I was impressed with Luna's ability to stand up and ask for clarification on things. But, more than that, I was in awe of how she went toe to toe with this man. All I expected from her was to take notes on things he and I talked about. But, as we headed to the last property of the day, I quickly found that I was the spectator in this match.

And Luna was about to be the lightweight champion.

"Personally, Miss Faircloth, this last property is my favorite. It's got five different well sources from which it draws its water, yet the sewer is tied into the city of Conroe. The electrical grid is stable. In fact, I can produce paperwork as to the work that was done on it a couple of years back. This is the only property that is still owned by the original purchasers, and while it's a bit smaller than the other ones we've looked at, it's got the least amount of work that has to happen."

I nodded. "Then, let's get inside this bad boy and take a look."

As we traveled inside the last warehouse, a thought occurred to me that could screw things up: I enjoyed spending time with Luna. I enjoyed having her at my side. I enjoyed watching her go for the jugular. I enjoyed listening to the sound of her voice and feeling her presence at my side.

The issue? I was now her boss, which made any personal fraternization even more complicated.

"There's insulation behind these walls, right?" Luna asked.

Mr. Derecho walked alongside her down the hallway. "Yes, ma'am. All of the hallways are insulated, as are the walls to every space that make up the outer perimeter of the main building. There are three stories to this portion of the property, all of which are insulated and have their own air units."

"Nice, nice. What about expansion? Are we primed in this location to add what we need?"

As their voices trailed off down the hallway, I let my eyes sweep over Luna's body. Her plump ass filled out the fluttering floral dress she wore as her hips swayed with every step. She had her hair pulled back in curled wisps that made me want to run my fingers through it.

I can't believe she's not off-limits.

"You're an idiot, Bart," I murmured to myself.

Luna was just as gorgeous today as she was back at the cookout when we reconnected again. Her devotion to her family was something I respected about her. Still, her uncanny ability to launch herself straight into a position like this with confidence and coolness about her left me speechless, just like the sloping curves of her hips did.

"Fuck," I whispered.

I jogged up behind them and tried to act as if her smile and her mind hadn't completely disarmed me. But, when she grinned at me from over her shoulder, I knew she had caught me. All I did was toss her a playful wink, and she shook her head, but I knew if I did anything else, I'd be pushing the envelope.

Then again, my entire life had been built on pushing the envelope.

"So! What do you think?" Mr. Derecho asked.

The three of us made our way back to our vehicles as I drew in a deep breath. "I think we have some talking to do, but you'll be hearing from me by tomorrow morning."

My realtor nodded. "I'll be on the lookout for that phone call. And in the meantime, I'll start digging up other properties if none of these suit your fancy."

Luna shook his hand again. "We'd appreciate that, thank you. Mr. Remington and I will probably chat over dinner, so I expect you'll hear from us sometime tonight."

My eyebrows rose. "Dinner, huh?"

She looked up at me. "I mean, unless you want to go talk about it right now. But, I figured you'd want to take my notes, show them to your brothers, and digest everything first."

"No, no, no. Dinner is just fine."

Mr. Derecho chuckled. "I'll be waiting either way. And Miss Faircloth?"

"Yes?"

My realtor pointed at me. "If he's stupid enough to get rid of you, I want you to call me. I could use someone like you on my team."

She giggled. "I'll take that into consideration."

I interjected, "But, it won't be necessary."

We waved my realtor off before I walked her over to her

car, and I managed to get her door open before she dipped down inside. I backed away as she slid the keys into the ignition, anxious for tonight to come around.

But, when she turned her car over, nothing happened. I furrowed my brow as she tried cranking her car again, but it did the same thing. She did it again and again until she sighed and stepped out of her car.

"Maybe the alternator's sticking. Do you have an umbrella or some sort of long stick in your truck somewhere?" Luna asked.

I walked around to the bed of my truck. "I've got a pipe around here somewhere that I use for the same reason. Pop the hood of your car, and we'll figure it out."

I laid my hands on that pipe just as she propped up the hood, and I lowered the pipe down to where the alternator was. I knocked against the metal object softly, hoping to dislodge it so Luna could at least get herself home. But, the engine still wouldn't turn over. Not even trying to jump her car with my truck's battery worked.

"Seriously?" she whispered.

"Luna, let me give you a ride home."

She sighed. "I appreciate that, but that still doesn't solve my problem. That's the only car I've got, other than my father's truck. And I can't take that from him."

I opened my passenger-side door. "Just let me get you home, and we can figure out the kinks later, okay? We can discuss that over dinner as well. Maybe I can talk to the company and see about getting you a company vehicle."

She looked up at me. "You'd do that for me?"

I shrugged. "It wouldn't be the first time we have issued someone a company car, so I don't see why not."

She climbed into my truck. "Thank you so much."

"You're more than welcome. I'll make sure you're taken care of."

By the time we got back to her apartment, it was damn near dinner time anyway. I parked my truck in the dimly lit parking lot and looked over at Luna, who seemed to be deep in thought. And without thinking, I placed my hand over hers to try to comfort her, which pulled her gaze over to mine.

"We're going to figure this out, okay? I'll have your car towed this evening to the nearest garage so it's not sitting out there waiting for someone to come across it."

She sighed. "I can't thank you enough. I'm so embarrassed."

I squeezed her hand. "Don't be embarrassed. Do you know how many times my truck has stranded me somewhere? It could be something as simple as the gas gauge being broken or something as serious as an engine issue. Either way, it happens to the best of us."

She snickered. "Guess this is a 'no' on dinner, then."

"I mean, we could order something in and talk. Do you need help unboxing boxes or anything like that?"

"Nah. Just clothes I have to put away."

"Well, the offer for dinner still stands. We need to talk about these properties anyway. Might as well do it over food."

Her eyes fell to our connection. "I suppose you could come up if you don't mind chaotic messes."

I chuckled. "I have two brothers. Chaotic messes are my life."

Her giggle washed over me, and my heart beat rapidly in my chest. It was the most incredible sound on this planet, and when her eyes met mine, I saw her eyes slowly widening. The black of her pupils swallowed up the beautiful, crisp golden eyes she had, and my stomach turned itself into knots.

Just kiss her. You know you want to.

"Luna?"

"Yes?" she asked breathlessly.

"What would you like for dinner?"

And before I could even start tossing out options, her lips crashed against mine.

Answering my question with a need that stiffened my cock against my jeans.

❧ 8 ❧

Luna

Him. I wanted him for dinner. I'd wanted Bart since he first sat down at the table my father and I shared at the cookout months before with his button-front shirt and his jeans that clung much too tightly to his frame.

And dammit, I'd wanted him ever since he came knocking on my door, checking up on me after what happened at Pete's Chicken.

His hand cupped my cheek and ran straight through my hair. I climbed across the seat, wanting nothing more than to be closer to him. He tasted of coffee and strawberries, an intoxicating meal I wanted more of. And as my tongue slid against the roof of his mouth, I felt his hand draw away from my hair before wrapping around my waist.

"Get over here," he grunted.

In one fell swoop, I was in his lap, blocked in by the steering wheel. Straddling his pelvis as I felt his thick erection pressing through his jeans. His hands slid up my dress, cupping the backs of my legs as he showed me exactly how he wanted me to move.

And when my hands fell to his belt, he moved to help himself out of his jeans.

I kissed down his neck as he growled and groaned my name. The sound alone shot shivers of heat throughout my entire body, ravaging my very soul as my heart took flight. It had been so long since I'd been with a man. Years upon years of nothing but self-pleasure and dreams to keep me going during the lonely nights. But, as I stroked Bart's thick dick, feeling his precum slicking his skin, his fingertips effortlessly slid my damp panties off to the side before I raised my hips and hovered over his cock.

"Luna."

My eyes fluttered open, and I gazed into his darkened stare. "Yeah?"

"Are you sure this is something you want?"

What a hunk. "More than anything."

His hands gripped my hips, and he dropped me down, sliding my wet walls against his girth. Moans poured from my lips as my forehead fell to his shoulder, allowing the electricity of his touch to take me under. I gasped as my hips bottomed out against his body, his thickness filling me so incredibly that it felt like the first time.

His fingertips dug into my skin, marking me even before I started moving.

I raised my head from his shoulder and found his stare again. His eyes, half-hooded in pleasure, sparked a need in my gut that was much too strong for my helpless desires. I rolled my hips, watching his eyes roll back as his hands moved me exactly how he wanted me. And as I swiveled my hips, his thumb dipped inside my panties, parting my pussy lips. There was no room to move, but somehow, he made it work.

"Oh, shit," I hissed.

"There it is," he growled.

I bucked harder against him. "Bart. Oh, God. Please."

"That's it, Luna. Take what you want. Own what you need."

I whimpered, "Holy fuck."

His thumb pressed against my clit as I ground against him, feeling his cock pulse against my walls. I bucked heatedly, bouncing his truck on its chassis as his free hand gripped my hair. He pulled back my hair and sank his teeth into my neck, sending shockwaves of pleasure through my veins.

And just like that, my body burst. "Bart!"

He grunted. "Shit, Luna. Yes. Milk that dick. Fuck, I'm so close. So close. Yes. Right there. Just—ugh."

I collapsed against him, panting for air as I felt his cock explode. Strings of arousal filled me to the brim before my pussy pushed him out. The evidence of our arousal fell against his seats, marking his truck with our scent. And as I breathed him in deeply, my face pressed into the crook of his neck, I felt him wrap his strong arms around me as we quaked with the aftershocks of our orgasms.

He kissed my forehead in such a tender fashion that I almost wasn't sure it had happened. My body settled against his, our hearts beating rapidly in time with our panting breaths. The world tilted around me. I closed my eyes and felt the axis of the world shifting back and forth, reminding me of the joy I just experienced.

The joy of fucking my boss.

My head ripped up from his shoulder. "Oh, no."

Bart shifted. "What?"

Reality crashed into me as quickly as my pleasure had, and I felt myself panicking. "No, no, no, no," I murmured.

Bart furrowed his brow. "What is it? What's wrong?"

I pushed myself away from him. "I, uh…"

"Luna, look at me."

He tried to take my hand, but I moved farther away. "I need food. Bad. It's making me sick."

"Well, here. Let's get up to your apartment and we can—"

"I just need to be alone, okay?" I looked over at him and saw his eyes boring into me.

"Are you sure?"

I swallowed hard. "More than anything."

He sighed. "At least let me walk you up."

I watched him stuff himself back into his pants, and it hurt more than I wanted to admit. I fixed my hair and my clothes, trying to make myself look presentable as my entire body burned with embarrassment. I had just had sex with my boss. I did the one thing I always told Willow not to do.

I'm a hypocrite.

"Luna, wait!"

I let my body do what it needed to do without my mind interfering. I grabbed my purse and pushed open Bart's truck door before leaping out. I made my way for the outside stairs that led straight up to my second-floor apartment, my heart slamming against my chest as Bart kept calling out my name. I leaped up the steps two by two, unwilling to wait for Bart lest it prolonged the embarrassment I felt churning tears behind my eyes.

And after slamming the door behind me, I let the tears fall as I listened to Bart's truck sputter to life before driving away.

"Dammit," I whimpered.

I wiped at my tears and dug around in my purse before I speed-dialed the girls. I knew they'd give me shit—especially Willow—but I needed to talk with them. I needed their advice. My mind remained clouded with a mixture of shock and ecstasy. I'd never had a man make me feel that way before, and of course, that man was my boss.

I mean, we'd even been on the clock!

"Hey, hey, hey! The kids are eating, and I've got some free time," Willow said.

Sadie groaned. "I'm just lying here. I feel like shit."

I sniffled. "Thanks, you guys, for picking up."

Willow paused. "What's wrong?"

Sadie's voice grew stronger. "Who am I killing?"

I giggled breathlessly. "I, uh... I've made a massive mistake."

"Do you need me to come over?" Willow asked.

"You can come to pick me up before you go. *Will!*" Sadie exclaimed.

I walked over to my couch. "No, no, no. I just—I need you guys to tell me it's all going to be okay."

"Has something happened with your father?" Willow asked.

"Will says I'm good to go," Sadie said.

I put my head in my hands. "So, Bart offered me this job, right?"

"Oh! Yeah! Today was your first day, right? Bryce was telling me about it," Willow said.

"Will! Why didn't you tell me Bart hired Luna!?" Sadie exclaimed.

I pinched the bridge of my nose. "It went fine until my car died in the parking lot of a refinery place we were looking at. He had to drive me home."

"Is... that what's wrong? Your car?" Sadie asked.

"You didn't," Willow said.

I felt the tears brewing again. "I don't know what to do. Bart's my boss, you guys. H-H-He—"

"Can someone fill me in?" Sadie asked.

The call fell silent as I drew in a deep breath. "Bart and I just had sex in his truck."

Sadie scoffed. "Well, it's about damn time."

"You know, I was sitting here just thinking that," Willow said.

I blinked. "What?"

"Oh, come on," Sadie giggled. "I saw the chemistry you two had at the barbecue."

"How your father's attitude just rolled right off his back," Willow said.

"I'm honestly surprised it took this long to happen, really," Sadie said.

I shook my head. "I don't get it. This isn't a bad thing? He's my boss now, you guys."

"And?" Willow asked.

Sadie barked with laughter. "You would."

I rolled my eyes. "Can we focus? I'm having a crisis over here."

Willow started laughing. "If you're still this panicked, then you need to get laid more. You're supposed to be relaxed after, not more wound up."

"You guys, this job is only temporary for me," I said.

Sadie clapped her hands. "Even better! Then, once you have to quit, you won't feel bad about banging him anymore."

I flopped back against the couch. "Guys, I'm being serious right now."

Willow sighed. "So are we. You're making a big deal out of nothing. I mean, you two were practically attached at the hip at the cookout. I see the way he looks at you. None of this shocks me one bit."

I blinked. "Wait, how does Bart look at me?"

"I love you, Luna, but you've always been so clueless," Sadie said flatly.

I scoffed. "Hey..."

Willow clicked her tongue. "She's right, though. You're so hung up on the fact that you now work with him—"

"For him," I corrected."

"Whatever. For him. You're so wrapped up in that part that you can't even admit what a good thing this is. You like him, right?"

I paused. "I mean, he's handsome."

"Come on, Luna. If you're going to work through this, then stop lying," Sadie said.

I leaned back. "All right, all right. Yes. I *like* the man. But, that doesn't matter because he's off-limits now. Or, he should have been. And besides, if this refinery doesn't work out? He goes back to Houston, and I'm left here. I can't just leave Conroe, especially with my father's condition. This job is temporary for both of us, and then we go back to our lives. That's how this is going to work."

"That's how you *think* this is going to work," Sadie said.

Willow cleared her throat. "She's right. This could all go according to plan, and the refinery keeps Bart here. Then, what?"

I shrugged. "Then, he's still my boss, and nothing changes either."

"Can I ask you something?" Sadie asked.

I sighed heavily. "I know you will, anyway."

"Why do you always attempt to jeopardize something good that comes your way?"

Willow jumped in. "That's actually a really good question. You're terrible with that shit, and you need to stop."

I furrowed my brow. "I do not."

"Uh-huh, yes, you do," Sadie said. "Remember Michael?"

I rolled my eyes. "Michael was a musician. He would've been gone too much."

"And Brock?" Willow asked.

"Too young. I thought it was kind of weird for me in the first place. I like men older than me, not younger," I said.

"And Ricky?" they asked in unison.

I swallowed hard. "All right, okay. I get it."

"We love you, girl," Willow said, "but you're a commitment-phobe."

I balked. "I am not!"

"Yes, you are. And the sooner you admit that, the sooner you can figure out why," Sadie said.

"You always find little ways to discard the men who find you attractive; who really do care. And then you end up going on dates with men like that asshat from the gas station. I don't know what you feel you're protecting yourself from, but Bart's about as good of a man as you're going to get. All of the Remington brothers are. And if you can find fault with him? Then, the issue isn't with him. It's with you," Willow said.

I closed my eyes. "Thanks for talking with me, I guess."

"We love you, but sometimes it has to be a tough kind of love," Sadie said.

I licked my lips. "Love you guys."

"Don't give up on him just yet, okay? Promise me," Willow said.

"And me," Sadie said.

I shook my head. "I'll try my best."

"That's all anyone can ask," Sadie said softly.

As I hung up the phone call with the girls, I thought back to my childhood. Bart had always been the one to stand up for me, especially with bullies on the playground. I'd been bullied for my weight my entire childhood, at least until the boys around me hit puberty and realized having a massive ass wasn't a terrible thing after all. He'd been just as protective of me as my father had been. But, he always had aspirations of getting out of Conroe, starting his own business, and finding his own home.

His leave from Conroe again wasn't just an eventuality; it was set in stone by him. It had always been his dream to set up somewhere else. Somewhere a bit bigger with more entertainment and more nightlife. So, I needed to protect myself in whatever form that protection came. Not because Bart was a bad man, but because he wasn't a forever man.

And that had to be taken into consideration.

9

Bart

"Luna, do you have that paperwork for property number four? I'm trying to crunch numbers and—"

She rolled her chair toward me. "The stack of folders to your right is all to do with that property. The top file is past bills, middle two files are contractors quotes and information to make necessary changes, and the bottom file is filled with the schematics and blueprints of the property."

I peered over my shoulder. "You getting hungry? It's almost lunchtime."

She rolled back over to her desk. "Already ordered! I figured pizza would be a good way to go since we probably aren't at an actual stopping point."

"Nice. Did you get—"

"A three-meat for you with red peppers? Yes. I also got myself a separate one because I'm a—"

I grinned. "Veggie pizza person."

She giggled. "Yep. I guess you know."

I murmured to myself, "I know more than you think."

She swiveled around in her chair. "What was that?"

I matched her movements. "Nothing. Just talking to myself."

"I do that a lot, too. Especially in—"

"The shower?"

She snickered. "I win all of my best arguments there."

The two of us just clicked. All week long, we'd been working side by side in my hotel suite, trying to crunch the numbers of these places. None of them really stuck out to me, but Mr. Derecho was giving us the space we needed because we were now faced with a decision as to which of the six properties would suit us best. It would cost way too much money to build a refinery from scratch, but a great deal of these properties needed so much work that we might as well have done exactly that.

And all the while, my chemistry with Luna mounted.

Every day she worked with me, I found another reason to be amazed. With each passing hour, her perfume filled my nostrils and invaded my workspace, tugging at my cock as I tried to keep my desires at bay. Neither of us had brought up what happened the other evening, and part of me didn't want to. We'd gotten back into a comfortable rhythm, and I didn't want to do anything to ruin that. But dammit, I needed this woman.

And not just professionally.

It gutted me that she wouldn't even consider making this a permanent position for herself. But, I was on a mission to change that. I knew I'd never find another assistant who I worked so smoothly and so diligently with, whether or not we had slept together. Work didn't feel like work whenever she was around.

I have to find a way to get her to stay.

Our pizza arrived, and we ate while we worked. We passed folders back and forth, updating numbers and trying to total out the closest number we could for our investors. I needed portfolios to them by the beginning of the week, and that meant getting these numbers and the names of these contractors as accurate as possible.

But, once the day wrapped up, I had everything I needed to give the investors what they wanted. "You're a powerhouse, Luna; you know that?" I swiveled around in my chair just as she got up from hers.

"Well, if there's nothing else for the day, I should be getting—"

I stood to my feet. "You've technically completed your first week back at work."

She paused. "It doesn't even feel like a week, does it?"

I snickered. "No, it doesn't."

She smiled up at me. "I really want to thank you for this

opportunity. It's going to change a lot of things in my life for the better."

I slid my hands into my pockets. "If you're up for it, I'd like to take you out and celebrate the success of your first workweek."

She grinned. "Or, you're just sifting for platonic reasons to take me out because of what happened last week."

I shrugged. "Then, if you don't want to go out with me, a simple 'no' will suffice."

Her eyes danced between mine, but her lips didn't move. A smile grew against my cheeks, and when she smiled back, I knew we were on for the evening.

"Give me fifteen minutes, and I can give you a ride back to your place, and you can get changed. I just need to slip out of these clothes and into—"

Luna furrowed her brow. "Why would I want to get changed? Do you not like my dress?"

My eyes fell down her body. "I love everything you wear. But, I figured with my brothers and the girls coming out with us tonight, you might feel like changing. You certainly don't have to, but I thought you might want to."

She smiled so big that her eyes almost closed. "You already know me too well."

"And I consider it an honor."

When our eyes met, it was as if I couldn't look away. Like someone had my head locked into that position and Luna was holding me hostage. My God, she looked incredible in the sunlight streaming through the windows of my hotel suite.

And had she not freaked out so badly on me last week, I would've led her right to my bed and had dessert before dinner.

But, I kept my cool. "Fifteen minutes, and I'll be ready."

Luna cleared her throat. "Yes. Yes, uh, well, I'll be here."

After getting changed and hopping into my truck, Luna and I headed for her apartment. I kept stealing glances at her as she gazed out the window, her body pressed as close to the door as she could get. It killed me inside, knowing she regretted what happened between us. Because I thought what happened was beautiful. And I knew damn good and well we both enjoyed it.

Having her once is better than not having her at all.

The sentiment only served to hurt my soul even more, though.

"Oh, my God," Luna gasped.

I pulled into her parking lot. "What? What is it?"

She threw her door open. "My front door is open!"

I looked up at her door. "Luna, wait!"

She took off running, and I didn't even turn my truck off. I jumped out and raced up behind her, wrapping my arms around her waist. I picked her up and pulled her off the steps as she kicked and tried to wiggle away from my grip.

"Let me go! What if something's happened?"

I set her down and spun her around. "And what if someone's broken in? What if they're still up there?"

Her eyes watered. "That's just what I need after my car breaking down."

"Let me go up first. I'll clear it and then poke my head out. Okay?"

She nodded quickly. "Okay. I'll call the police."

"Good idea."

As she dug out her cell phone, I inched my way up the stairs. I slid my hand into my pocket, pulling out the pocketknife I always carried with me. I mean, it was no shotgun, but it was something. And as I slid my way into Luna's apartment, the chaos around me stopped me in my tracks.

Luna hadn't just been robbed. Her entire place had been trashed.

"Come out if you're here! There's no other way out!" I exclaimed.

I walked into the middle of her living room and turned myself around.

"Bart?" Luna asked.

I flipped my knife closed and slid it into my pocket. "It's clear. Just... brace yourself."

She peeked her head around the corner. "Oh. My. God."

The second her eyes started watering, I rushed to her side. I took her in my arms as she clung to my shirt, her tears wetting the fabric. It burned my blood that someone would do this to her. That someone would intrude upon a space that was supposed to be sacred for the sake of some selfish want. I pulled her over to the side as sirens wailed in the distance. Police cars and a fire truck came screaming into the parking lot before a familiar face started up the steps.

"Andrew," I said.

My high school friend nodded. "Bart."

Luna lifted her head. "You two know each other?"

Andrew held out his arms. "Don't tell me you don't remember me, Lunapad."

She blinked. "Lanky Andy?"

He chuckled. "Well, most people call me 'Officer Rinkinson' now, but that'll work."

Luna pulled away from me. "I don't know what happened. We just pulled up after work, and my door was hung wide open."

I rubbed her back. "I came up here to see if anyone was still here, but it was empty."

Andrew nodded as another pair of officers slipped into the apartment. "Well, Luna, if you don't mind walking around with us, we could use your set of eyes. If anything was taken, you'll know it when you don't see it."

I looked down at her. "You up for something like that?"

She wiped her tears away. "Anything to catch who did this to my home."

Andrew held out his arm. "Right this way. You start wherever you feel comfortable, and we'll follow behind."

I stepped out onto the small landing in order to give everyone a bit of space. But, I kept my eyes glued to Luna. As she walked around her studio apartment, I saw her arms cross over her chest and her shoulders slump. She'd gone from the confident, headstrong woman I knew her to be and had turned into a scared, self-conscious little girl.

I wanted to wring the neck of the person who had done this to her.

"Is there anyone that you know who could have done this? Someone you've had a bad encounter with or something?" Andrew asked.

I almost hopped in until I heard Luna sigh. "Well, there is this one guy."

Andrew pulled out his notepad. "What's his name?"

I slipped back inside and stood behind Luna, wanting to provide a bit of support. But, when she leaned back into me, part of me was shocked. But, part of me was honored that she felt comfortable enough to seek out my touch.

As she rattled on about the guy from Pete's Chicken and how they had met, her one hang-up was the fact that the man didn't know where she lived. He'd never come over. He had never driven her anywhere. It was just one failed date before she stopped returning his calls. I knew what the internet was capable of, though, and the information someone could dig up if they checked the right places.

And when the police officers were done logging all of the damage in her apartment, Andrew sighed.

"We're going to check security footage and see if there's something to go on, and we'll follow up with this guy. Since Bart here called the police, he shouldn't be hard to track. I'll stop by or give you a call if we come across anything, but in the meantime, do whatever you can to keep yourself safe. Even if it means going and staying somewhere else for a little while."

I snickered. "Or getting yourself a new boyfriend."

Luna's eyes whipped up to mine. "What was that?"

I shook my head. "Just a joke. I didn't mean any harm."

"Wait, wait, wait, what was the joke, though?"

I shrugged. "Usually, people like this are more prone to staying away from places when they know there's a man involved. If you were targeted, you could've been targeted because you're a woman who lives alone. I was just making a joke about getting a boyfriend to scare off anyone else who might get any other ideas."

Andrew chuckled. "You always had the worst timing with jokes."

I rolled my eyes. "Guess some things never change."

One of the officers came rushing back inside. "Sir, you need to see this."

Andrew took the outstretched phone from his co-worker before turning it to face Luna.

"Is this the man you were just talking about?" he asked.

Luna leaned forward before she nodded. "Yeah, that's him."

Andrew groaned. "Yeah, we're very familiar with him. He's currently living in a camper at a local campground, and this isn't the first time girls have reported issues with him."

Luna paused. "He told me he lived—"

"Off Battleground and Lynn Drive?"

She swallowed hard. "That's not where he lives?"

"It's where he lived four years ago before he was evicted."

Luna sniffled. "How could I have been so stupid?"

I placed my hands on her shoulders. "It's not your fault. Men like him are very good at getting women to turn their heads his way. It's just what they do."

She shook her head. "I should've been smarter than that. I've always been smarter than that."

Andrew handed the cell phone back to his co-worker. "Chances are he's already found another campground to hang out in, so we'll go searching around. He usually never travels far, so we'll catch up to him sooner or later."

Luna sighed. "At least you know who the guy is. That makes me feel better."

I clicked my tongue. "Well, it doesn't make *me* feel better."

The more we talked with Andrew, the more this "fake boyfriend" scheme seemed to make sense. I mean, the two of us worked together anyway, so it wouldn't be too hard to convince someone that we were together since we spent hours of our days together in the first place. If I could get Luna to agree to it, then it wouldn't be hard to fake, either. I already liked her. I already thought she was fantastic. But, in the end, it all came down to her.

And whether or not she felt she'd have to fake too much in order to paint a believable picture.

🙎 10 🙎

Luna

Everything felt like such a whirlwind. One second, I was headed home to get changed for a nice dinner outing, and the next second, I was standing in front of Willow and Bryce's place with bags at my feet.

And when I looked over at the person rubbing my back, I found Bart looking down at me with a soft smile. "There you are. I was wondering when you'd come back to earth."

I blinked. "What's going on?"

He cocked his head. "Do you remember agreeing to stay with Willow and Bryce for the night?"

Willow took my hand. "We've got the guesthouse all nice and set up for you."

Bryce nodded. "And the guest bedroom is ready upstairs if you'd rather stay in the main house."

I looked around and saw Sadie here, too. Will stood behind her with concern in his eyes, and suddenly, the weight of the world crashed against my chest. I drew in deep breaths through my nose, trying to calm myself as much as possible. It was hard, though.

"I'm sorry. I don't—remember much after the police left," I said softly.

Bart chuckled. "So, I take it you don't remember me agreeing to stay with you, then."

My eyes whipped up to his. "What?"

"In the guesthouse out back? I told you that if you were going to stay out there, then I'd stay with you so you wouldn't be alone. And you insisted on staying in the guesthouse so you wouldn't—"

"Be a burden," I whispered.

Sadie gripped my shoulder. "You can also come to stay with us. We don't have as much room as Willow and Bryce do here, but what room we have, you're more than welcome to it."

I shook my head. "No, no, no. The guesthouse is fine. I—thank you."

Willow snickered. "Girl, you don't have to thank us for shit."

Will walked off the porch. "Your bags still in the truck, Bart?"

I turned around. "Bart doesn't have to stay with me. I promise I'll be fine."

Bart's voice sounded in my ear. "Not a chance. If you stay in that guesthouse, I'm staying with you. And I'm not taking 'no' for an answer."

I was much too tired to fight with him, so I threw in the towel. Will hoisted both of Bart's bags from the bed of his truck as Willow and Bryce gathered mine from my feet. And while I knew my father wouldn't be happy about an arrangement like this at all, especially since I could just go stay with him and his twenty-seven million guns, the idea of being around Bart comforted me.

I felt safe with him.

We all walked around back, and our bags were plopped in the middle of the guesthouse living room. Sadie walked into the kitchen and started making coffee while Will got on his phone and ordered us all food from the best steakhouse in town. I walked over to the bay window at the far end of the living room and sat down on the cushion, gazing out at the horses across the way as they freely grazed and danced around.

I was envious of their freedom.

"Luna?"

I jumped at the sound of Bart's voice. "Holy shit, you scared me."

His face grew concerned. "Which is why I want to stay. You can't be this jumpy and expect to get sleep or be productive."

I swallowed hard. "I know. I know. I just..."

He grinned. "You're used to being the caretaker."

I nodded slowly. "Instead of being taken care of, yes."

"Well, if you want, I can leave my clothes strewn everywhere and expect you to do the dishes every day."

I snickered. "If I wanted that, I'd just get married."

"Hey, now! I only leave my socks lying around," Will said.

"And your nasty-ass boxers!" Sadie exclaimed.

I barked with laughter as Willow brought me a mug of coffee, and I was thankful for the warm feeling it brought to my numb hands.

"Thanks," I said.

She smiled. "Of course. You want to sit?"

I sipped my coffee. "I'm too anxious to sit."

Will walked over. "Food will be here in about an hour. You guys want to eat here, or in the main house?"

Bart looked down at me. "Luna? Where would you prefer to eat?"

I peered back out the window. "Why don't we all eat by the pool?"

Sadie giggled. "We can make it a pool party!"

Willow clapped her hands. "I've got a new bikini I've wanted to try out."

Bryce grinned. "Lucky me."

I rolled my eyes. "Willow, can I—?"

She grabbed my hand. "Borrow a swimsuit? Girl, of course, you can. Come on. I've got a yellow two-piece with gold trim that'll look great against your skin."

The dinner pool party was a rousing success, but I really wasn't hungry. I pushed my food around in the to-go tray and took a few bites, but I couldn't focus my mind enough to eat. Willow forced me to get into the pool for a bit before I dangled my feet in the hot tub with Sadie. And as the guys splashed us with cannonballs and soaked our towels, my mind kept swirling in all sorts of directions.

Until I looked up and saw everyone was gone.

Bart sat next to me on the edge of the hot tub. "You zoned out again on us."

I sighed. "I'm so sorry. I just—"

He took my hand. "You have nothing to apologize for. Though, I'm going to make you eat a little more before you head to bed."

I snickered. "If I had a nickel for how many times I've said that to people before."

He squeezed my hand. "How are you feeling?"

I shook my head. "How am I not feeling would be an easier question to answer."

Silence fell between us as the stars twinkled above our heads.

"I mean, I'm angry. Hurt. I feel stupid and embarrassed. I'm sad and frustrated, and I feel like every time I take a productive step forward, life always has a way of setting me right back in my place. Not to mention, when my father catches wind of what's happened and the fact that you're staying here with me? He's going to want your head on a stake."

Bart chuckled. "You let me worry about informing your father, and you just focus on things that'll help you ground yourself. Okay?"

"You don't know my father, though."

"Oh, but I do. I heard the stories when I was a boy. I know all about your father's intimidation tactics. But, when he understands that I'm staying here merely to make sure no one else comes after you, I think he's going to respond better than you think."

My cheeks puffed with my sigh. "You have more faith in him than I do, then."

"Luna, look at me."

I turned my gaze up to his. "Yes?"

He reached over and cupped the back of my neck. "I'm not going to let anything else happen to you. I need you to understand that. And I'll find a way to get your father to understand that. You just leave it to me, okay?"

I felt myself weakening to him. "Okay."

He grinned. "Plus, with me living here with you, it'll give off the impression that we're together. And that might make this guy—or whoever did this to you—back down. You know, knowing there's a man with you that he'll have to contend with."

I drew in a deep breath. "Or, it might make you a target."

He ran his fingers into my hair. "Well, that's a decision only I can make for myself, which is why I'm here with you right now."

Why does he have to be my boss? "I really appreciate that. A lot."

I felt more confused than ever before. As I leaned against Bart with our feet dangling in the hot tub, he held me close as his skin pressed against my own. On the one hand, my mind thought it might be okay since we really weren't together. But, my heart told me this was a bad idea for the exact same reason. What if we fell into a routine living together that I couldn't shake once the police caught whoever had done this? What if my emotions ran away with me, and I ended up falling for Bart when he was operating under the guise that this was simply a façade?

What if this is his way of trying to be my boyfriend long after this is over?

I wanted to ask him all of these questions, but my lips were too tired. My brain was too tired. And my soul was too hurt to delve into something so personal. "I'm really glad you're here," I whispered.

He laid his cheek against the top of my head. "I'm glad I'm here, too."

I closed my eyes and felt my body wanting to slip into a deep slumber. I felt myself relaxing against Bart's muscles, seeking out their comfort and their warmth as he started to shift my body. My eyes glued themselves closed as my body hovered in midair, and it wasn't until I heard the click of the doorknob that I realized Bart was carrying me back inside.

And just as he placed me against my bedroom mattress, sleep robbed me of my consciousness, where Bart continued to invade me in the form of my dreams.

❧ 11 ❧

Bart

I heard my cell phone vibrating on my bedside table and rolled over. With the sunlight streaming through the windows and the fan on the ceiling at full blast, I slapped my hand against the device and answered the phone call.

Here we go again. "Hello?"

"Mr. Bart Remington?"

I peeked an eye open. "Yes?"

"This is Colin Jackson, from—"

I shot upright in bed. "The contracting firm, yes."

He chuckled. "I'm sorry for the delay in my phone call. We had to jump through a few hoops before I could call you back."

I swung my legs over the edge of the bed. "No, no, no. It's completely fine. Tell me you've got good news."

He chuckled. "Oh, I've got great news. The evaluation of the bank for its renovations went very well, and very little updating to the interior electric and plumbing has to be done. We're cleared for all planned renovations, and demo starts in about an hour."

I leaped to my feet. "Holy shit! Yes!"

He barked with laughter. "Provided we don't come across anything major, renovations will take a couple of months."

"But, if we budget time for a couple of hiccups?"

"Three months tops."

I raked my hand down my face. "You have no idea how much I needed to hear that. Thank you so much."

"You're very welcome, Mr. Remington. It's a pleasure to work with your family. I have to say that this town is buzzing with the rumors of the refinery coming here. It'll mean a lot of jobs to people who have been out of work for a long time. And the vintage bank will be the perfect place for your office space."

"That's one of the problems we're hoping to tackle with the plant and this new office headquarters."

"Well, let me know whenever you start taking applications because I've got a cousin who's a single mother of three who could really use a job."

My heart broke for him. "Send over her resume and I'll make sure it's at the top of the pile."

"Really?"

I smiled. "Really."

"Oh, man. Thank you, seriously. This is going to give her a lot of hope."

"It's the least I can do. And again, thank you for calling."

After I hung up the phone with the contractor, I crafted a group text to send to my brothers. My fingers moved as quickly as they could, given the fact that I was very un-caffeinated. I walked into the bathroom and sent off the text, ready to splash some water in my face.

But, before I could even get the faucet turned on, I remembered my brothers and I had a coffee date planned for nine sharp.

We had a lot to talk about. Furnishings for the office building, for one. We needed to draw up a list of how many people we needed to hire on the spot as well as their job titles. We needed to speak with our medical insurance company, the investment firm that housed our retirement accounts, and we needed to hire an interior designer to really lay out our office space and make it feel professional while also feeling like home.

And we can put our headquarters in Houston up for sale.

After splashing water onto my face and hopping in for a quick shower, I walked out of the bathroom with a towel wrapped around my waist. I silently walked up to Luna's bedroom door and eased it open, peeking into the darkened bedroom. Even though the morning sun streamed slightly through the cracks around the blinds, her soft snoring made me grin as her shoulders steadily lifted and sank with her breathing.

So, I took great precautions to keep myself quiet as I got ready for my day.

"I take it you have some good news for me?" Bryce asked.

I walked into the main house, and the smell of coffee greeted me. "Let's wait for Will, so I don't have to repeat myself."

I heard the front door open. "Don't worry, everyone! The party has arrived. And I come bearing gifts of bagels and cream cheese."

Bryce licked his lips. "If we're going to have those, I'll need to fry up some bacon."

I snapped my fingers. "Do you have any more tomatoes from the garden?"

Bryce pointed. "Slice up a few while I fry this bacon up."

Will dropped the bag of food onto the counter. "Should I whip up some eggs for the kids when they get up?"

I smiled. "Might as well whip up a whole dozen in case anyone else wants some."

Bryce turned on the stove. "So, what's this good news you have for us?"

Will interjected. "Willow not up with the kids yet?"

I shot him a look. "Really, dude?"

Will shrugged. "Just a question. They're usually up by now."

Bryce chuckled. "It's okay. They're actually all piled in bed right now. Willow had to get up in the middle of the night to chase some nightmares away, so they're all tangled up in my comforter, trying to catch up on some rest."

My heart leaped at the mental image that was painted in my head. I wanted to have a life like that one day. One where a beautiful woman bore my children and helped me create a home where we could all thrive and love one another unconditionally. In some respects, I was incredibly jealous of what my brothers had.

Maybe Luna feels the same way.

Will nudged me. "The hell you smiling about over here?"

I chuckled. "The fact that I got the call from the contractor this morning."

Bryce's head whipped toward me. "And?"

I snickered. "Demo begins within the hour."

"Holy shit!" Will exclaimed.

Bryce clapped his hands. "Hot damn, it's actually happening."

Will wrapped his arm around my shoulders. "You know what this means, right?"

I nodded. "Yep. We can put that stupid building in Houston up for sale in order to foot the down payment for the refinery."

Bryce nodded. "That's as big of a 'bingo' as we've ever had."

Will patted my back. "A celebratory mug of coffee sound good to everyone?"

I started slicing tomatoes. "Sounds perfect to me. But,

make it quick. I'm liable to cut off my fingers if I don't get some caffeine in me."

Will fixed up our coffee while Bryce and I whipped up a quick breakfast. Then, after everything was cooked and ready, we sat down at the kitchen table. We started drawing schematics and rough sketches on paper napkins and jotted down ideas of interior decorations to run by a designer. And after we outlined what jobs we needed to hire for immediately, Bryce placed the phone call we'd all been waiting to place for months.

Bryce put our Houston realtor on speaker. "Let me guess. This is the phone call."

Bryce nodded. "This is the phone call, Hamilton."

I heard him clapping on the other end of the line. "It's about damn time. I've got people crawling all over me about that building!"

I blinked. "Wait, really?"

Will chuckled. "Oh, we're gonna have this place sold in no time."

The realtor started shuffling around. "Actually, I've got three offers already pending. We might be able to get this place sold before it even hits the market."

Bryce shook his head. "You're a fucking miracle worker, Hamilton."

Will leaned toward the phone. "Shoot Bryce the three offers in his email, and we'll get back to you on how we feel about them."

I nodded. "Yeah, let's make this happen."

We heard the realtor typing away. "Already on it. Try to get back to me before lunch, though. There's one offer in here I think you guys are gonna really like, but the clients have been hounding me over getting back an answer. Sooner is always better, in this case."

Bryce nodded. "You got it."

We hung up with the realtor, and I took a long pull from my coffee mug. I closed my eyes and relished the great accomplishments that had already taken place during the first hour of my day. I felt more relaxed than I'd felt in nearly a year. Moving our headquarters and opening this refinery had become a hefty process, and I'd lost sleep more than anything else over it.

But, when I opened my eyes, I saw my brothers staring me down. "What?" I asked.

Will snickered. "What do you mean, 'what?'"

Bryce scooted his chair closer to me. "You know what we're about to ask."

I blinked. "I'm half a mug of coffee in. Help a brother out."

Will chuckled. "You moving back?"

Bryce nodded. "Since this headquarters thing is panning out?"

I clicked my tongue. "Just because the headquarters is panning out doesn't mean the refinery will."

Will rolled his eyes. "Still making up excuses, I see."

Bryce reached for a piece of bacon. "Look, we all know

you wanted to get out of Conroe for a while and see the world, or some shit, but it's time to come home."

Will nodded. "Yeah, our entire business is here."

Bryce chomped on his bacon. "And your family is here."

"Not to mention your nieces and nephews."

I smiled at Will. "And the ones on the way."

Bryce drew in a deep breath. "How is Sadie anyway?"

I plucked a bagel from the bag. "Yeah, has her nausea finally dissipated?"

Will leaned back. "Unfortunately, no. But, she's only a few weeks out from her due date at this point, so it won't matter then."

Bryce shook his head. "What a miserable feeling."

Will chuckled. "You wouldn't know it by the smile she wakes up with, though."

I pointed at him. "That's a good woman right there. Don't ruin shit with her."

Will held up his hands in mock surrender. "Trust me; I'm doing everything in my power to make sure she and our twins are going to be happy for the rest of their lives."

Bryce patted his back. "Good man."

And for a split second, I felt my jealousy ebb to the surface. But, I stuffed it down quickly.

We had too much to accomplish now that things were finally rolling along.

"Well, if you need help finding a place, let me know," Will said.

Bryce threw back the rest of his coffee. "Same here. And you know you can always have that patch of land right here on Rocking R Ranch if you just want to build a place of your own."

Will nodded. "And I really suggest that you do. That way, you can create whatever you want."

I snickered. "I appreciate it, but one step at a time. Okay?"

The longer we talked about my moving back, the more I thought about Luna. Maybe if I moved back, Luna would be more than willing to stick around as my assistant permanently instead of only temporarily. Maybe that was the issue from day one: the fact that she believed my presence in Conroe was only temporary.

You still have work back in Houston, though.

I shook those nagging thoughts away from my head and focused on the enjoyment of the present. I mean, Luna and I hadn't even talked about what went down between the two of us in my truck, much less about anything else. I knew the conversation would come eventually, though. While I knew she'd be content with acting as if it didn't happen, I couldn't live my life like that. Eventually, I'd have to talk about it. And then, I'd get all of my answers at once.

"Earth to Bart, you there?" Bryce asked.

Will barked with laughter. "He's terrible with that shit now."

I drew in a short breath and leaned back. "I need more caffeine."

Will reached over and plucked my mug from my hands. "Coming right up."

The offer Bryce had for me in terms of building on the ranch was a generous one. But, I wasn't sure if I was ready to give up all of the hard work I'd put into my career as a geologist, working not only for my family but for many other Texas and Louisiana petroleum firms. It had taken countless hours of hard work and sleepless nights to position myself the way I had. And if I played my cards right, I'd be situated to take over the entire company I had helped to build once the owner retired at the end of next year.

Was I ready to throw all of that away for the family business?

Will placed my coffee in front of me. "Let me say one thing, and I'll leave it be, okay?"

I sighed. "Shoot."

Will sat down. "I know you like your job in Houston. And I know you always dreamt of being a geologist. But, all of the refinery properties you've looked at have been in Conroe, right?"

I nodded slowly. "Right."

Bryce interjected. "And you had a chance to look at refineries in Houston, but you didn't, right?"

I blinked. "Right."

Will grinned. "Then, it seems like all signs point to this refinery coming to Conroe."

Bryce patted my back. "And since your area of expertise is in the petroleum industry, you'd be the one running the refinery. The rest of us here have only been overseeing the oil leases that pertain to our land here in Conroe."

I looked over at him. "Yeah, you're right."

Will reached across the table for a slice of tomato. "Then, you better figure out something quick. Because all signs point to you moving back home."

And as we heard the pitter-patter of little footsteps coming down the stairs, Bryce turned his attention to his kids, while I sat there with my coffee growing cold, trying to sort out my future.

❧ 12 ❧

Luna

I stood on the back patio beside the pool, silently wiping tears from beneath my eyes. I knew it. I knew this job would only be temporary. Even with all they were celebrating, Bart still couldn't give a solid answer as to whether or not he was moving back.

I'd heard all I needed to hear.

I turned my back to the house and started walking to my bedroom in the guesthouse, but I paused. If I didn't show up for breakfast, someone would come looking for me. And their first question would be to ask me what was wrong. I peered over my shoulder at the house and looked through the kitchen window, watching as a tired Willow fussed around with the kiddos.

Then, I saw the guys get up and start hugging a very pregnant Sadie.

I drew in a deep breath and sighed before I rolled my shoulders back. I needed to put on a brave face, even if I didn't feel that brave. I wiped away the last of my tears and shook my head, tossing aside all of those thoughts that rattled me to my core.

Then, I turned on a dime and headed straight into the house.

"Luna!" the guys exclaimed.

Sadie embraced me tightly before Willow handed me a mug of coffee.

Bart stood from his chair. "Here, you can have my seat."

I waved my hand at him. "It's fine. I feel like standing for a little while, anyway."

"Are you sure?"

I nodded. "I'm very sure. But, thank you."

Will gestured his arm over the table. "There's a plethora of foods for you to try."

Bryce wrinkled his nose. "Since when do you use the word 'plethora?'"

Sadie giggled. "Since I taught it to him."

Everyone fell apart with laughter, and I did my best to join in. But, I felt Bart's eyes on me, studying me as if to pick my every move apart.

Does he know the laugh is fake?

After Willow retrieved an extra chair for me to sit in, I wanted to scratch her eyeballs out for placing me right next to

Bart. Then again, she'd always been a meddler, and I shouldn't have expected anything less. I sat down and felt the heat of his body radiating against my own, so I lost myself in the smooth, rich blend of coffee as I lifted my mug to my lips.

Chugging, and swallowing, and trying my best to drown out his heat.

"You know, it's been a while since we've all sat down to eat together," Bryce said.

Will snickered. "Pretty sure the last time we did it, it was just us brothers."

Willow giggled. "Well, get used to it. Because once Bart moves back, we're doing this a lot more often."

I peeked over at Bart to watch his reaction, but all he did was dive into his plate of food.

Unwilling to engage. Interesting.

"Anyway," Sadie said, "I'm glad we're all here."

Will nodded. "Yeah, it's good to have family back together again."

I glanced over at Bart again, but he kept his eyes down-turned toward his food. He practically shoveled it into his mouth and covered his face with his coffee mug. Anything to keep his eyes away from us.

Dodgy son of a bitch.

"Luna," Willow said.

"Hmmm?" I asked.

"Did you sleep okay last night?"

All eyes were on me as I drew in a deep breath. "I tossed and turned a bit, but I think I got enough rest."

Bryce reached behind Bart and squeezed my shoulder. "Anything we can get you?"

I sliced into a tomato. "You guys have done enough. This is just going to take some time, is all."

Will swallowed down his mouthful of food. "Well, if you need anything, don't hesitate to ask."

I need Bart to stay in Conroe. "I definitely will, thank you."

The thought that rolled across my brain shocked everything inside of me except my heart. And I hated myself for it. Why did I always have to go for the unattainable guys? Why did I always have to set my sights a little too high? I wanted to get up and storm away from the table. I wanted to smack Bart across the face for stringing me on.

Then again, it wasn't all his fault. I was the one who threw myself at him.

Idiot.

Willow sighed. "Sweetheart, come on. We've talked about this. Food doesn't go in your diaper."

Bryce pointed with his fork. "See that? That's what you're getting into, Will."

Will barked with laughter. "Bring it on."

Sadie leaned back in her chair. "Ugh, it's been a long time since I've eaten that much."

Will started rubbing her belly softly. "Let's pray it stays down this time, yeah?"

Bryce got up to go help Willow while I watched Will and Sadie stare into each other's eyes. I wanted that someday. A family, a partner, and a man who would look at me as if I were his entire world. I blinked back a few tears and took a bite of my cold scrambled eggs, trying to distract myself from the world that surrounded me.

Why do they get to be happy, but I don't?

"Hey, you okay?" Bart asked.

I looked over at him and saw concern in his eyes. "Yeah, I'm okay. Why?"

He held up his phone. "I have to slip away for a second. Just wanted to make sure you were good."

My heart plummeted to my toes. "Oh. Yeah, yeah, I'm good. You don't have to stay by my side all the time. Go to what you need to do."

"You sure?"

I forced myself to nod. "I'm sure, yeah."

"All right. Thanks." He picked up the phone and stepped away from the table as I let out a heavy sigh.

I pushed my half-eaten plate of food away and drained the rest of my coffee into my stomach. I wanted to hide away from the world. I wanted to coop myself up until this hell I'd found myself in finally passed.

You need to be happy for your friends.

It wasn't that I wasn't happy for them. I just wanted what they had for myself. I wanted children and a home, a man who loved me, and a kitchen table all my own to fill with the family we created together. I wanted my father to actually like a guy I had a crush on instead of frightening them away and adding to my loneliness.

But, more than that, I wanted my own slice of happiness.

Even if it still came with that loneliness.

"You okay?" Sadie asked.

She reached across the table and took my hand as the guys started clearing the table.

"Yeah, yeah. I'm fine. Just—I'm so tired, you know?"

She squeezed my hand. "I can imagine."

I snickered. "Of course, you can. You're—what?—five weeks out?"

She smiled. "Four, as of yesterday. The doctor actually said the twins could come at any time and everything would be fine."

Willow sat down next to me, holding her little one up to her breast. "I'm so excited for you."

Sadie released my hand. "Honestly? I'm about ready to cut them out myself. I'm over this unrelenting nausea. And my hips are killing me."

I giggled. "I bet. Have you and Will settled on names yet?"

Will piped up from the sink. "We haven't decided."

Sadie shook her head. "We really haven't settled on names yet."

I shook my head. "Well, maybe it'll be one of those moments where you look at their sweet faces, and their names just come to you."

Bryce barked with laughter. "Yeah, right. Pat and I debated over Marie Lee's name for days before we came up with one."

Willow grinned. "Yeah, apparently, 'Marie Lee' was 'baby number one' for a week after they brought her home."

Sadie's jaw dropped open. "You're kidding."

Bryce reached for my dirty plate. "I'm really not. So, don't be like Pat and me. Settle on the names now."

Everyone nodded, but I couldn't even bring myself to fake my participation. I wasn't sure if I'd ever get away from the family dynamics long enough not to be jealous. Sadie looked like she was about to burst from the fullness of her joy, and Willow still had that sparkle in her eyes almost two years into her relationship with Bryce. It made me sick with envy. I wanted what they had, but everything in my life worked against me when it came to obtaining it.

Maybe my destiny was to be alone for the rest of my life. Or, maybe I was nothing but a supporting character on the main stage of the lives of the Remington family. Either way, it made me sick to my stomach. So, I softly excused myself and booked it back to the guesthouse as quickly as I could move.

❧ 13 ❧

Bart

I muted my deep sigh. "Well, I appreciate the call, even though the news isn't fantastic."

Mr. Derecho clicked his tongue. "Don't discount the other three properties, though. Just because those three have come off the market doesn't mean—"

"I know, I know. I'm just frustrated that the three left require the most work."

"If you can get the headquarters in Houston sold, however, you'd have the money for a nice remodel, even after you put down a down payment."

I chewed on the inside of my cheek. "I have a lot to think about. Can I call you back?"

"Do you want me to be honest?"

I blinked. "Don't tell me you have buyers for the other three properties already."

"I told you these things would go quickly, especially with how business is booming in your area. Your company put Conroe back on the map, but that comes with consequences."

I wanted to growl at the man. "How long do I have before I need to make a decision?"

"Ideally, yesterday."

My face fell. "Ha. Ha. Ha."

"I can try to hold these properties another few days, but after that, I have to start showing them to people. This isn't just costing you money; it's costing me money."

"I know, I know."

I was angrier at myself than anything. Every second I continued to waffle around would cost me more than I had bargained for. And now, after solidifying the renovations for our new headquarters, it felt like I was back at square one with finding a place for the refinery.

I slid my hand through my hair. "Let me call you back after dinner tonight. I want to clue my brothers in and get their opinions."

Mr. Derecho sighed. "I'll keep my phone on me."

"I appreciate it, thanks."

As I hung up the phone, I turned and found Will staring at me. He had his hands on his hips, and his brow squinted like Mom always did whenever she was trying not to pry. It made me grin, thinking about Mom.

Dad would know what to do.

But, just as Will stepped off the front porch and headed toward me, the one number I never wanted to see roll across my phone screen popped up. And I braced myself as I picked up the phone call from our bank.

"This is Bart," I said.

Will motioned for me to put it on speaker as the woman on the other end of the line started talking.

"Am I speaking with Bart Remington?"

Will nodded. "And Will Remington."

Bryce jogged up behind me. "Also, Bryce."

The woman giggled. "I'm glad I've got the three of you here. I have some news."

I puffed my cheeks out with a sigh. "Let me guess. Not the best kind of news."

She snickered. "It's... a bit of a roadblock."

Bryce took my phone from my hand. "To whom am I speaking?"

The woman cleared her throat. "My apologies. My name is Caroline Branfield. I'm a loan officer with—"

Bryce interrupted her. "Is something wrong with our loan application?"

"That's why I'm calling, yes."

My head fell back. "What do we need to fill out now?"

Will nudged me as Bryce shot me a look. "What my brother means is, what's the next step?"

Caroline's words made me cringe. "There are no last steps, actually."

Will blinked. "So, we have the loan?"

She paused. "I'm afraid not."

I groaned as I put my face in my hands. "Fucking hell."

Bryce cleared his throat. "Is something wrong with our paperwork, Miss Branfield?"

She started shuffling papers around. "It's not about your paperwork, Mr. Remington. It's about your assets. For the loan you're requesting, the three of you don't have enough collateral to offset the balance of the loan should the bank have to foreclose."

Will snickered. "Well, that's never going to happen. I'm sure our father's—"

She interrupted him. "It doesn't matter. Mr. Remington. When the bank orders an appraisal, it's to make sure the bank isn't making a bad investment. And while your business records and credit scores are impeccable, you still don't have enough collateral for the bank to feel at ease in giving you the loan amount you're asking for."

A thought occurred to me. "What if we lowered the amount of the loan?"

Bryce leaned over to my ear. "We can't afford a higher down payment."

I waved him away. "According to our assets, what dollar amount for the loan are we eligible for."

I heard her typing away at her desk before she spoke. "The loan would have to be amended to somewhere between 2.5 and 3.5 million."

Will whispered. "We'd need at least a million more, and that's for the 3.5."

Bryce sighed. "We could see if Uncle Ryan might be willing to front us the money."

I felt my heart drop to my toes as I shook my head. "No, he's got enough on his plate right now with things. Can you reprocess our paperwork for that loan amount?"

"I can certainly amend it, but the process will start all over. It'll go back to your loan officer where he'll check all the papers, the three of you will have to sign amended documents, and then the loan will have to go back into underwriting."

I was ready to pull my fucking hair out. "That sounds wonderful. We'd greatly appreciate it."

"Great! I'll keep you updated via email, but I'll get this paperwork back to your loan officer. You should be hearing from him by the end of the day."

I nodded slowly. "I appreciate it, Miss Branfield."

"Of course. I'm sorry it wasn't better news. Good luck!"

We're going to need it. "Thanks."

Bryce hung up the phone and tossed it back to me as Will stretched his arms over his head.

"So, prematurely celebrating hasn't ever really been our style," he said.

I rolled my eyes. "We don't need jokes. We need ideas. How are we going to come up with the other million?"

Bryce shrugged. "We'll easily have it with the selling of the building in Houston."

I shook my head slowly. "I don't think we should bank on that just yet."

Will paused. "Why not?"

"Before that call, Mr. Derecho called me. Our top three properties are already off the market."

Bryce rubbed the back of his neck. "You're kidding."

I shook my head. "Nope. So, the money we get from the sale—"

"—is going to have to go to improvements and remodels. Just fucking grand," Will said.

Bryce groaned. "What if we posed the issue to our investors?"

I scoffed. "And risk them backing out? We'd be screwed if that happened. No, no, I'm not comfortable tipping those scales."

Will shook his head. "Then, what the hell are we going to do?"

Bryce placed his hand on my shoulder. "How long do we have to decide from the three remaining refinery properties."

I chuckled bitterly. "I told Mr. Derecho I'd call him back before dinner."

"Jesus," Will whispered.

I shrugged. "The only way I see this panning out is if I go back to Houston to personally oversee the loan process so I can find other realtors in the area."

Bryce furrowed his brow. "Realtors? Why?"

I held out my arms. "Look at what just happened! In the blink of an eye, we lost our top three properties. And I'm sorry, but none of the other three properties are anywhere near what we need. Our only hope is to find an abandoned refinery or something either in Houston or on the coast. And that requires me to travel back."

Will shook his head. "We were supposed to bring this business back to Conroe. We promised Dad we would."

I shrugged. "Well, sometimes shit doesn't pan out the way we want."

I looked back at the house and saw Willow standing on the porch with the kids. Sadie stood there with her hand on her back and her other hand planted on the top of her rotund stomach. But, Luna was nowhere to be found. I knew that if I had to go back to Houston, I'd be gone for days. Possibly weeks. And while I knew I needed to tend to my office and my career there, I didn't like how much time I'd be spending away from Luna.

I turned to Bryce. "If you came with me to Houston, we could knock this out in three weeks. I'm sure of it."

He shook his head. "I can help from this end, but Willow needs my help here with the kids."

Will nodded. "Especially now that Sadie's about to pop."

Bryce motioned to Will. "And he can't go for obvious reasons."

I started grasping at straws. "I mean, he'd only be a thirty-minute plane ride back."

Will glared at me. "Are you serious right now?"

I raked my hands through my hair. "Well, I'm sorry you two decided to run off and play house in the middle of us expanding our family's company. But that wasn't my decision."

Maybe Luna's right.

Bryce put his hands on my shoulders. "We can always put this off a year or two."

Will ruffled my hair. "Yeah. We can always put this on hold—or press pause—until we have our feet underneath us again."

Maybe this thing between Luna and me was always supposed to be temporary.

"No, no. It's fine. I'll go to Houston and work it out," I said.

Bryce looked into my eyes. "Are you sure about that?"

I shrugged. "That's the only way it's going to get done. And we promised an entire town we'd find a way to make this work. Even if the refinery doesn't come here, we still have our new headquarters here, which will bring our conferences with it."

Will nodded. "That'll breathe a least a little bit of life into this place."

I continued with my train of thought. "And eventually—when we do expand—we can expand to one of the smaller properties here. Or even build our own. The refinery plant doesn't have to be built here. There are other facets of the business we can always bring to Conroe."

Bryce murmured. "But, that'll keep you in Houston. Away from family."

I shrugged. "Sometimes, you gotta do whatcha gotta do."

But even though I tried consoling my brothers, what they didn't know was how quickly my mind was racing. How much my palms were sweating. How much my heart was breaking.

What they didn't know was that I had started to regret every decision I'd ever made that had brought me to this point.

14

Luna

Every time I went out somewhere, I felt myself looking over my shoulder. Every time I made a trip somewhere, it felt like everyone was staring at me. Every sound in the dark made me jump. Every creak in the floorboards made my eyes water. I hated feeling this way. I hated feeling so scared and so paranoid every time I left the guesthouse and traveled out into the world.

So, I decided to call Dad.

"What?" he asked as he answered the phone.

I giggled. "Having a good morning, I see."

He grumbled. "Hey there, El."

"Hey, Dad. How are you feeling?"

"Fine. How's the apartment?"

Guilt swarmed my gut. I didn't want to lie to my dad, but I also didn't want to tell him the truth. I knew someone would die by his hands if I did. I just didn't know if it would be that stalker guy or Bart. And I didn't want him to hurt Bart.

"I'm actually spending some time with Willow and Bryce," I said.

"Oh? Everything all right?"

I shrugged. "Yeah, they're good. I mean, they just need some help. Bryce is working more than ever on some refinery project or whatever, and Sadie is too pregnant to help out anymore."

"How's she feeling?"

I blinked. "Willow or Sadie?"

"Both, I guess."

I smiled. "Willow's overwhelmed and missing Bryce, but good. Sadie's ready for her pregnancy to be over, though."

"She still sick a lot?"

I sat down on the couch. "I don't think she threw up yesterday, but she's just picking at food for now."

"So, probably trying to avoid throwing up."

"Probably."

"They know what the twins are yet? Or are they being weird and making it a surprise?"

I giggled. "A few days ago, Sadie finally forced Will to give in."

He chuckled. "Let me guess. Two boys?"

I blinked. "How did you know?"

"Women are always sick as hell with boys."

"Like you'd know."

He clicked his tongue. "So, when you gonna stop lying?"

I froze. "What?"

"There's something you ain't tellin' me. What's going on?"

I sighed. "Dad, it really is okay."

"Luna, you're my daughter. I know when you're withholding something. Now, tell me what's going on."

"I'm handling it. I swear, it's okay."

His voice lowered. "I ain't gonna ask you again."

I stood to my feet. "And while I'm still your daughter, I'm also an adult. So, you need to trust me when I tell you that I have it under control."

Silence fell over the phone before I heard Dad draw in a curt breath. "I'm here if ya need anything. Okay?"

I blinked. "Yeah, I know."

"Good. And call more often."

I smiled softly. "Can do."

"Love you."

"Lo—love you, too, Dad."

He chuckled. "Sure about that?"

I smiled. "It's the one thing I'll always be sure of."

"All right. Talk soon."

"Yeah. Talk soon."

I hung up the phone before the front door inched open, and through the slat of the door, I saw Bart's twinkling eyes.

"Sorry, didn't want to interrupt," he said.

I waved him in. "No worries. I understand."

He came and sat beside me on the couch. "We have a lot to get done in a small span of time. So, we'll be working in overdrive for a few days."

I cracked my knuckles. "Ready when you are."

Bart had been off the past few days, but once I did some digging into the documents he wanted me to read over and the phone calls I placed on his behalf, I quickly figured out what was happening. The headquarters was coming along splendidly, but the buildings we had picked out for the refinery had already been sold off to the highest bidder. My heart went out to him. Bart seemed more stressed than I'd ever seen him before. But, I also knew what all of this might mean.

He'll have to go back to Houston.

Bart typed at lightning speed. "I'm moving the video conference you just scheduled back a day. I'll need that time to go look at some places along the coast."

I nodded. "I just got your meeting with the bank scheduled. It's next Monday at nine."

"Perfect. For how long?"

"Slated for an hour, but they said they'd block off two hours just in case you guys needed it."

He continued typing away. "Perfect. We're probably going to need every bit of those two hours."

After scheduling meetings and setting up his schedule for the next month, the last thing I did was schedule his flight out in the morning. He was adamant about flying back and forth instead of driving, and while I didn't ask why, I was curious.

Was he trying to make it seem like he was going to come back?

Stop giving yourself hope, Luna.

"Can I ask you something?"

I nodded when Bart's voice pulled me from the recesses of my mind. "Sure. What's up?"

He chuckled. "Can you look at me for a second?"

I leaned closer to my laptop. "Just one more... thing... and... got it! Submitted." I turned to face him and found a solemn look on his face. "Everything okay?" I asked.

He rubbed the nape of his neck. "So, I've been thinking."

Uh oh. "About what?"

"About you, and us, and this job you've taken so well to."

Fuck, fuck, fuck, fuck. "It's a great job. I'm very thankful for it."

He grinned. "I know. And I could really—"

I felt myself slipping and falling into the beautiful pools of his adoring eyes. "Yes?"

He clicked his tongue. "Come to Houston with me. Help me there. As a team? We could knock this shit out in two, three weeks."

I felt my stomach drop to the floor. "Oh."

He blinked. "Oh?"

I cleared my throat. "I mean, no. No, I—I can't do that."

He took my hand. "Luna, you are so efficient. You make this entire process damn near seamless. I could really use you on that end."

I slid my hand away from him. "You know I can't go, Bart. I have to stay here in case something happens to Dad. I'm all he's got. You know this."

"I could hire some in-home care for him while you're gone."

I shook my head. "It's not going to be the same. He's weird about strangers."

He chuckled. "The man's sixty-two years old. I'm sure he's just fine with strangers. Especially if I hire a nice-looking nurse for him."

I scoffed. "Contrary to what most people think about my father, he's got a few better morals than that."

He paused. "I'm sorry. I didn't mean to offend you. It was only supposed to be a joke."

I stood to my feet. "Well, it wasn't a very funny joke."

I folded my arms over my chest and walked over to the window. I gazed out over the rolling pastures, watching as their beautiful horses galloped and frolicked and rolled around in the grass. They seemed so carefree and happy. Like their lives were completely worry-free.

Lucky them.

Bart's voice sounded behind me. "Will you at least help me from here, then?"

I caught his eyes in the soft reflection of the window. "I was already planning on it. This is my job, remember?"

He nodded slowly. "Yes. Right."

I snickered. "Is it five o'clock? Because I could really use a drink."

He grinned. "One tall glass of wine and a fruit and cheese plate, coming up."

I went back and sat on the couch as Bart prepared our snacks and drinks. He came over and sat beside me, handing me a glass full of wine with a skewer of fruit sitting across the top of the glass. I leaned back and took a long pull of the cold liquid—until my pull turned into a chug.

Before I knew it, all the wine was gone and my body started to meld with the couch. I drew in a deep breath through my nose as Bart plucked my glass out of my hand, making his way to the kitchen to refill it. I wasn't sure how long he was gone or when he sat back down. But, when I felt his shoulder brush against my own, I looked over at him.

And I found his eyes dancing between mine.

"What can I do to help?" he asked.

I furrowed my brow. "Help with what?"

He took my hand again. "Whatever it is that's got you wound so tight."

Don't do it. Don't do it. Don't do it. "Nothing appropriate, I'm sure."

He grinned. "Well, technically, we're off the clock."

I rolled my eyes. "Typical man."

"Which means I'm not really your boss right now."

My gaze searched his face. "Then, what are you right now, if not my boss?"

His face leaned closer to mine. "Someone who cares and is concerned."

And this time, I knew damn good and well what I was doing when I pressed my lips against his.

15

Bart

The second her wine-soaked tongue fell against my own, I couldn't contain myself. I slid my arm around her back and shifted her on the couch, guiding her back to the cushions. Her lips caught my fall as our teeth clattered together. Her hands raked through my hair as I pawed at her clothes.

I wanted all of her. I wanted to feel every single part of her.

And I wouldn't stop until I got what I wanted.

"Bart," she moaned.

I slid my lips down her neck. "Dammit, you make me feel alive."

Our clothes came off in a frenzy before I wrapped my lips

around her puckered nipple. She arched her back against me, parting her legs as my cock stiffened and ached for her warmth. I kissed down her stomach. I traced the peaks and valleys of her curves with my tongue. But, before I could settle between her legs, her hand gripped my hair.

And she pulled me up to her face. "I need you. Now," she said breathlessly.

My cock fell between her pussy lips. "As you wish, beautiful."

I pulled back and sank myself deeply into her body, watching as her eyes fluttered closed. I grunted and growled, feeling her tightness overwhelm me as my balls pulled up into my body. Not yet. I wasn't ready yet. I wanted to mark this entire guesthouse with her scent before I filled her to the brim. But, she started bucking, and I couldn't contain myself.

"Holy fuck," I growled.

I sat back on my haunches and pulled her closer to me, watching her curves jiggle for my viewing pleasure. She gripped the couch cushions, accepting my intrusion as I pounded against that beautiful pussy of hers. I watched her juices coat my skin. I felt her arousal dripping down my aching balls. And as electricity overwhelmed my body, I felt her walls collapsing around me.

"That's it! Bart! I'm coming. Please. Don't stop!"

I tossed her legs over my shoulders and folded her in half. I rutted against her like a wild beast, gnashing my teeth and allowing the euphoria to overwhelm me. Her nails raked down my arms. I felt her hands wrap around my wrists. And as my hips began to shutter, I felt my cock explode, coating her walls with my mark.

"There it is. That's it. Oh, shit. Luna. Fucking hell, Luna."

Her trembling legs slid from my shoulders, and I collapsed against her. Her tits pressed against the divots of my chest as her arms lazily wrapped around my neck. I kissed her skin. I peppered them along her bare shoulder. But, when I pulled out my cock, a gush of fluid rushed from between her legs, making her giggle.

"I need a shower."

I kissed the crook of her neck. "I can do you one better."

She groaned as she shifted beneath me. "What do you mean?"

I pressed my lips to her ear. "Bryce and Willow took the kids to her aunt's place for the night."

With her eyes sparkling with mischievous delight, I slid off her body. I scooped her into my arms, even though my body was weak from the pleasure she had afforded me, and I carried her naked body out to the pool. The closer I got, the faster I moved until I was jogging with her in my arms. Her tits bounced, and her face was tucked against my neck as she clung to me.

"Bart!" she squealed.

"Geronimo!" I exclaimed.

I leaped into the pool with her in my arms, feeling the chlorine wash us down as we went under. The water swallowed us whole as we swam around underneath the setting sun, clad in nothing but our skin. Luna splashed me, and I splashed back. She swam toward me and did somersaults underwater while I watched her beautiful body enjoy the life it was living.

Every time she popped up from the water, she planted the softest kiss against my lips. And every time she did it, I wished with all my might that we were actually a couple.

"Luna?"

She grinned. "Yes?"

I reached for her, pulling her closer to me. "Do you ever wonder what it might be like if we were actually together?"

Her eye twitched. "What?"

I wrapped my arms around her waist. "Have you ever thought about what it might—?"

She interrupted my statement with a kiss, and I was too weak to fight. I hadn't nearly had my fill of her, and I quickly hoisted her out of the water. She gasped in shock as I effortlessly lifted her, setting her down against the concrete side of the pool.

Then, without another word spoken, I parted her luxurious thighs.

"Oh shit, Bart. Right there."

Her hand fisted my hair as my tongue fell between her pussy lips. The hairs on the back of my neck stood on end as I finally tasted her the way I wanted. She bucked against my face, coating me in her slick juices as I eased a finger into her tight entrance. And when she propped her heels against my shoulders, the sun finally set over the treetops.

Allowing the stars to twinkle above our heads. As if they were clapping and cheering us on.

"Right there. Right there. Oh, shit. Harder. Harder. Suck on that clit, Bart. Oh, yeah, baby."

I reached down into the pool and started stroking myself with my free hand. I pumped Luna's pussy full of my fingers as I spread my tongue against her clit, allowing her to use my face as she wanted. I felt my cock growing in my palm. I felt her body quivering with her orgasm as I swallowed down every last drop of her.

And when she collapsed against the pavement, I pushed myself out of the water.

"My turn," I growled. I straddled her face as I stroked my cock, watching as her half-hooded eyes looked up at me. I grinned down at her as I gripped her hair in my hand, watching and waiting for her to be ready. Her eyes lit up with the darkness. The moon hung heavily in the sky as her hands slid up my thighs.

Then, she sat up and motioned for me to lay down before she wrapped her plump lips around my dick.

"Oh, God," I grunted.

She slowly swallowed until she gagged around my length, and fucking hell, the feeling shot me into the sky.

"Dammit, Luna, you're perfect."

She whimpered around my dick, and I knew I wouldn't last long.

"That's it. Suck that cock. Hollow out those beautiful cheeks, Luna."

Her hand wrapped around my base, and she quickly bobbed her head. Her tongue swirled around my tip, lapping up my precum as I fucked her face. I grasped her hair and guided her motions, propping myself up on my free arm just so I could watch her work.

And when she finally took me all the way in, I cupped the back of her head.

"I'm coming. Luna. Goddammit, you're incredible. Don't stop. Just like that. Oh—fuck—"

My back fell to the pavement as my balls finally unleashed. For the second time that night, I filled Luna's body with my arousal as it shot in thick strings from my cock. My thighs contracted and released. My balls pulled so deeply into my body that I thought they might never return again. And as she cleaned me up with her tongue, I found myself gazing up at the crescent moon, hoping—and praying—that things worked out in our favor.

"Luna, I just..."

She crawled up my body and silenced me with another kiss. But, I wouldn't fall for it this time.

I spoke in between her kisses. "Luna. Please. We have t—mm."

She giggled. "All you have to do is lie there, okay?"

I shook my head. "No, no. Luna. We really need to ta—"

I felt her palming my cock. "You ready for round three?"

I pushed myself up. "Luna. Stop."

She shook her head. "I can't, Bart."

I blinked. "You can't what?"

She sighed. "I can't do this. I can't have this conversation with you right now."

I reached out for her. "Come lie next to me. We can stargaze before we—"

She stood to her feet. "Not tonight. I can't tonight. I'm sorry."

"What?"

She sniffled. "I'm sorry, Bart. I'm just not that strong."

And as I watched her rush back into the guesthouse, I felt like we had taken four steps back instead of one step forward, causing me to wonder if she and I would ever be on the same page.

❧ 16 ❧

Luna

I looked over at Bart in the passenger's seat. "You got everything you need?"

He scooped his carry-on bag up from the floorboard of my rickety car. "Yep, I got everything. Plus, I've still got my place back in Houston, so all of my clothes and things are already there anyway."

"Right. Well, call me when you land. That way, I'll know you're safe, and I should have some updates for you by that time."

He grinned. "You know it's Sunday, right?"

I shrugged. "You're flying to Houston to get ready for a busy work week, so I'm going to do a bit of overtime and make sure things on your end go smoothly with the meeting in the morning."

"Last chance to come with me. I can book another ticket."

I snickered. "Get out of here. You'll miss your flight."

I waved Bart off at the airport as he slipped out of my car. Then, I raced back to the guesthouse to get to work. I had a plethora of phone calls to place and answers I needed to questions Bart kept asking himself. He needed as much information as he could get going into these meetings this week, and the more prepared he was, the better chance he stood at getting what he wanted.

Which meant I might get what I wanted out of all this.

"Hello, my name is Luna Faircloth, and I'm calling on behalf of Bart Remington. Yes, I want to know how much the property is upfront and how much wiggle room there is to negotiate.

"The place has to be heavily ren—"

"Well, your client should have kept up the property. That's not my problem."

I listened as the agent prattled, and I got a little riled up myself.

"No, that's not what I'm asking. What I'm asking is for the exact dollar amount we would need t—yes. I know it's an estimate. But, get that estimate as close as you can get. That's what I'm asking for."

The agent pounded on the keyboard on the other end loudly enough for me to practically count the keystrokes before giving me an answer.

"Yes! Yes, that's exactly it. Thank you. I really appreciate it."

I soared down the list of phone calls I needed to place and jotted down answers to things in my notebook. I reached for my third lukewarm mug of coffee and threw the rest of it back, rejuvenating myself to try to get through the last hour of my workday. But, when I looked at the clock on my laptop, I paused.

Bart should've called by now.

I picked up my phone, and I didn't see any missed calls, which made me worry. His flight should've landed three hours ago. I took a break to check my voice messages, just in case he had called and my phone had hiccuped or something like that. But, I didn't have any voice messages, either.

I went to dial Bart's phone number, but my phone started ringing before I could. I drew in a deep breath and braced myself, hoping and praying it was him on the other end of the line. However, when I picked up the phone, I found myself talking to a contractor from the bank instead of Bart.

And the contractor wasn't happy.

"This is Luna Faircloth."

"Uh, yeah. Hello. This is Dave Hanbraum. I'm the team leader for the job at the bank."

I leaned against the couch. "Yes, Mr. Hanbraum. What can I do for you?"

"I was told to get in touch with you if I needed to get a message through to Bart Remington?"

You and me both. "I can definitely pass a message on. What's your message?"

"Can you let him know that there was a pipe behind the southern-most wall that has been steadily leaking, so we're going to have to remove the rotted wood and re-insulate? The job is gonna tack on another grand or two, but it has to be done."

I held back a groan. "I will definitely let Bart know."

"So, should I proceed?"

Shit, is this my call? "It doesn't sound like we have a choice, Mr. Hanbraum. Go ahead and proceed, and I'll let Mr. Remington know. And thank you for calling."

"Yes, ma'am. I'll let my team know. Thanks."

"And thank you for the call."

Just as I hung up the phone, a soft knock came at the guesthouse door. I tossed my phone onto the coffee table and pushed myself up, not really in the mood for entertaining company. But, I figured if it was Willow needing help with the kids, then the least I could do was help since they were letting me stay here, rent-free until my apartment was no longer a crime scene.

However, when I opened the door, I didn't find myself staring at Willow.

"Will?" I asked. I looked around to see if Sadie was standing there. But, he'd come alone.

"Is everything all right?" I asked.

He chuckled. "Why wouldn't everything be okay?"

I shrugged. "I don't know."

He glanced inside. "May I come in?"

I stepped off to the side. "Be my guest." I ushered him into the living room and was about to offer him a mug of three-hour old coffee. But, the determined look on his face had me much too curious. I closed the door behind me. "Something wrong?"

He clasped his hands behind his back. "I'd like to temporarily hire you for a job."

I grinned. "I already have a job that keeps me pretty busy."

"I'll pay you time and a half at the rate Bart is currently paying you. But, I need a bit of help, and you were the first person who popped into my mind."

I folded my arms over my chest. "Have you heard from him, by the way?"

"Bart?"

I nodded. "He was supposed to land, like, three hours ago. And I told him to call me when he arrived in Houston, but his phone keeps shooting me to voicemail."

He snickered. "His phone is probably dead. Bart is terrible with charging that thing, and flights make him tired. He's probably at his place taking a nap."

That'll have to be good enough. "All right. What's this job?"

"I just got done meeting with the interior designer for the bank, and I want to go ahead and get furniture orders placed."

"Is that the part you need help with?"

He shook his head. "I need help haggling prices a bit. Some of the stuff throws us a bit over budget, and those little 'bits' add up to about five grand over budget."

I whistled lowly. "That's a good chunk of money, considering the snag the bank just ran into."

He blinked. "What snag?"

I sighed. "A Mr. 'Braumhan' or someone called me not too long ago, saying there was a burst pipe behind the southernmost wall?"

"Oh, boy."

"They have to clear out the rotted wood and re-insul—"

"*Oh*, boy."

I cocked my head. "So, we might want to make the savings on this furniture and design a cool seven grand."

His eyes widened. "The new fixes are gonna cost two more grand?"

"Don't worry. I can easily save you that in furniture costs, and we might not have to haggle as much as you think. There's plenty of furniture out there that looks professional and comfortable and presentable without paying top-dollar for it. I'll make sure you save that money, okay?"

He nodded. "Sounds like a plan. Are you free tomorrow morning?"

I shrugged. "I'm free right now if the stores are open on Sundays."

He smiled. "Then, by all means, let me drive."

Will led me out to his truck, and we climbed in, but I still kept checking my phone. Even with Will's explanation, it had me really worried that Bart hadn't called me yet. I shook my head and kept my hand on my phone, just in case it started vibrating.

And as we pulled into the first furniture store parking lot, Will turned to face me. "Can I give you some advice?" he asked.

I whipped my head over to face him. "Huh?"

He nodded at my phone. "With Bart. Can I give you some advice with Bart?"

I furrowed my brow. "Why would I need advice?"

His face fell. "No one's stupid, Luna. We see how you two dance around each other. How you two look at each other."

I felt my cheeks flushing. "I don't know what you're talking about."

He rolled his eyes. "Well, I'm gonna give it to you anyway. If you really want to be with Bart, then go for it. But, this dance you two are doing is only going to prolong things and possibly sour things if one of you doesn't make the first move."

I slid my phone into my pocket. "We should get going inside. This place closes in an hour and—"

Will reached out for my wrist and grabbed it. "He's been unhappy in Houston for a while now."

I slowly looked back over at him. "He has?"

He nodded. "He hasn't said it in so few words, but he has been calling Bryce and me more frequently lately to rant and bitch about things. I think getting out of town as a young man wasn't what he thought it would turn out to be."

My heart ached for him. "Do you think he wants to come home."

Will slid his hand into mine and squeezed. "I think it wouldn't take much to make him move back home at all."

I felt hope blossom in my chest as Will released my hand. And together, we started into the furniture store. While Bart staying in Conroe for me sounded romantic and wonderful, I also didn't want to be the sole reason he returned. I mean, what if he came back and didn't like living here, either? He'd blame me for that. I'd seen that plot pan out too many times on television and too many times in real life with high school friends of mine to think that this scenario would be any different.

If I were the reason he moved back and shit went south, I'd be the first person he'd blame.

Maybe he'd even regret me in the process.

The thought made me nauseous, but I swallowed hard as Will opened the door for me. I raised my hand toward one of the store workers, and they waved at me before holding up their finger and going back to the client they were talking to —which, of course, gave Will more time to water the seed of hope I wished he hadn't planted.

"Just get out of your head and go with the flow," he whispered, "life's too short to try to control all of it."

I shook my head. "Can we talk about this later?"

"Will you willingly talk about it later?"

I shot him a look. "Do you have pictures of the furniture you're looking for?"

He handed me a small envelope. "All we can do sometimes is be tugged out to sea with the current that's sweeping us away. And honestly? Swimming against a current is almost a fruitless endeavor anyway."

I took the envelope from him. "In the ocean, though, swimming out of a current can save one's life."

His eyes lingered on my profile. "Do you feel like you need saving, Luna?"

I turned his question around in my head before I sighed. "No. I don't."

He patted my back. "Then, you've got your answer. Now, let's get this furniture ordered and get the hell out of here. I'm starving."

❧ 17 ❧

Bart

"Shit, for real?" I hissed.

I pulled out my phone to call Luna after I landed, and of course, it was dead. I cursed to myself as I booked it out of the airport and flagged a taxi down as quickly as I could. I dug around for my phone charger, hoping that the taxi driver would let me use their cigarette lighter to charge up my phone.

But, I couldn't find the damn charger.

"Are you kidding me?" I murmured.

"Sir?" the driver asked.

I sighed. "Can you pull over at the next pharmacy? I need to run in and get a phone charger."

"What about an electronics store?"

"If we come across one of those, great."

In a flash, the driver whipped a U-turn in the middle of a five-lane road, and I almost shit myself. I grabbed the "oh shit!" handle above my head and hung on for dear life as the driver tore across the street. With my eyes wide and my hands shaking, I walked inside and shelled out money for a charger. But it still wasn't one I could use in the car.

"Where to now, sir?" the driver asked.

I reached for the handlebar the second I dropped into the back seat. "I want to run by my office quickly and check on things. Then, we'll head to my place."

I rattled off the address of my office, and we booked it across town. I wanted to make sure things that needed to be done were getting done in my absence. And while I knew the office was filled with competent and passionate workers, I took extra care in the tasks given to me by the two men who still owned the company.

So, I wanted to make sure they didn't screw up.

"Bart! We weren't expecting you back so soon."

"How are things going with the bank?"

"Did you find a refinery for your family's business?"

"While you're here, can you take a look at this really quickly?"

What I wanted to do was get to my office, plug in my phone, and check on a few things. But, what ended up happening was completely different from what I had expected. Files were tossed at me, requiring my signature, and pictures of excavation sites were thrust in front of my face for commentary and efficiency suggestions. I scribbled notes into the margins of some files and crossed out a few things, signaling that the specific excavation tactic needed to be stopped.

And still, I hadn't gotten my damn phone plugged in.

Despite the signatures and giving my opinion on some things, though, there wasn't much I had to correct. I watched as everyone around me rushed back and forth between desks and jotted down notes, becoming more efficient with their time and suggestions with every second I was there.

"Hey, hey, hey. Mrs. Lila."

The salt-and-peppered hair secretary looked up at me. "Yes, Mr. Remington?"

I wiggled my finger around. "Is it always like this when I'm gone?"

She smiled. "It takes all of these people to do your job, yes. But I think they do it well. Don't you?"

Maybe they could keep doing it well while I'm in Conroe. "That's wonderful. And thank you for all you do."

She giggled. "It's my pleasure. Now, you get out of here. I have a feeling you're not in town to come back to this place yet, right?"

I winked. "You know me too well."

After leaving my office and finally getting back to my townhouse, I collapsed onto the couch. My head was swirling with so many questions and unanswered inquiries that the voices in my head lulled me to sleep. And when I woke up, I had a crick in my neck the size of Mars and a dead phone I *still* hadn't plugged in.

So, I heaved myself up off the couch, plugged my phone in, and dialed Luna's number.

She yawned as she picked up. "Bart Remington's secretary, how may I assist you."

I chuckled. "Assistant."

Her voice perked up. "Bart?"

"You're my assistant. Not my secretary."

She cleared her throat. "You know, I had to call the airline and make sure your plane landed safely and that you were on it before I could sleep last night."

Her sentiment warmed my heart. "I'm sorry. When I landed, I had to go buy a phone charger because I left mine back in the hotel. Then, I stopped by the office to oversee some things, and by the time I got to my place, all I could do was crash on the couch."

She giggled. "Will told me you were probably sleeping or something like that."

"How are things back at home? You have any updates for me?"

"Actually, yes. The team leader from the bank called and informed me of a two-thousand-dollar snag they ran into that they'd have to fix."

I pinched the bridge of my nose. "Wonderful."

"But, Will and I are saving a ton of costs on furniture and interior design. We've already saved three thousand dollars, and after today I think I'll end up saving you guys another grand."

I blinked. "He's paying you for your time, right?"

"Time and a half. And don't worry, it's not impeding the work I do for you. I'm glad I can help, though."

I smiled. "Anything else?"

"Eh, nothing to report that's major. Just some phone calls confirming appointments when you get back into town. The team leader wants to have a face-to-face, and Mr. Derecho has called me twice already. I told him I'd call him the second I heard from you."

I sighed. "That man is gonna kill us."

"He's trying the best that he can, but he does have buyers interested in those properties. Do you guys have any idea what you might do?"

I padded into my kitchen. "Call Bryce and Will and let them know that we need to do a video conference call during our lunch hour today. Mr. Derecho needs an answer from us, so call him back and let him know that he'll be hearing from me personally around one o'clock."

"Will do. Anything else?"

"Just keep being the wonderful human you are."

She giggled. "That isn't a problem, I promise."

I started making a pot of coffee. "Great. Now, I need to get off here so I can get ready for this meeting with the bank. I'll let you know how it goes."

"And I'll make sure your brothers are free for that lunchtime conference."

"You're the best. Talk soon."

"Yes, talk soon."

I hung up the phone and forced myself to walk upstairs so

I could take a shower and make myself look presentable. I felt myself running on fumes already, and it took me by surprise. Not once had I ever felt this tired and this worn down while I was in Conroe. But, less than twenty-four hours in Houston and I was ready to take a day off?

That didn't sit right with me.

Nonetheless, I chugged back some black coffee and put on my best suit. I made my way to the bank and arrived ten minutes before the meeting, where I came prepared with a portfolio of questions, signed paperwork, and blank sheets of paper to jot down notes. I couldn't walk out of this meeting without knowing damn good and well we could secure this loan. We couldn't keep going around and around until we settled on the magic number our assets afforded us.

And after thoroughly exhausting the bank representative, I had that magic number to give to my brothers at our lunchtime video conference.

"Three-million-one-hundred-and-twenty-four-thousand," I said.

Bryce's eyebrows rose. "That's honestly more than what I thought it would be."

Will shook his head. "It still doesn't put us in a good position, though. We'd still have to come up with—"

I interjected with the exact number. "One-million-three-hundred-and-sixty-thousand."

Will clicked his tongue. "Right. That number."

Bryce slid his hands through his hair. "If we place the

refinery around the Houston area, or just off Galveston, will that help us at all?"

I shook my head. "The whole point of building this refinery was to bring jobs back to Conroe."

Will shrugged. "I mean, it's not the only reason."

I glared at him. "But it's a real benefit. Guys, Conroe can't keep relying on seasonal rodeos to keep it afloat. There needs to be some sort of big business in the area unless we want our hometown to collapse and be just another small town that sunk."

Bryce leaned back. "We could open up a manufacturing plant."

My face fell flat. "For what? Parts we need for the refinery?"

Will blinked. "I mean, why not? If something goes wrong with the machinery, we're going to need to order out the parts anyway? Why not just keep it in-house?"

I shook my head. "Which is only going to mean more money we don't have right now."

Bryce pointed at me. "We've got the money, that's not an issue. The bank is just playing it safe right now because we don't have the reputation yet that Dad had with them."

I groaned. "That still doesn't help us now, Bryce. And we need help now. Plus, we've got our headquarters at the bank already underway. That'll be up and running in two, three months. What is that going to be for if we just agree to keep the refinery here?"

Bryce grinned. "You said it yourself: we could still hold our conferences here, and that alone would bring some money and temporary jobs into Conroe until we got our ducks in a row."

Will chuckled. "Or, are you having second thoughts about everything?"

I scoffed. "I don't know what I am anymore. But, I do know what our purpose is. And that's to bring this damn refinery to Conroe. So, we'll have to make it work."

Then, it hit me. "Wait a second, guys."

Will blinked. "Uh, oh."

Bryce chuckled. "Oh, I love this part."

I paused. "What part?"

Bryce barked with laughter. "The part where an idea hits you and you dig us out of this shithole."

Will leaned forward. "I'm ready to get out of this shit. Hit me with it."

I blinked. "Wait, seriously?"

Bryce rolled his eyes. "Come on, man. Spit it out!"

I held up my finger. "All right, but hear me out the entire way, okay?"

Will nodded. "Got it."

Bryce nodded in tandem. "Shoot."

I drew in a deep breath. "We've been trying to take out a business loan this entire time, and it's giving us nothing but a headache. But, what if we switched the kind of loan we take out entirely?"

Will narrowed his eyes. "Like, a conventional loan?"

Bryce's eyes widened. "You're kidding."

I sighed. "Just listen, okay? The three of us co-sign it, so all of our credit scores are pulled. We're all in the green, our personal assets aren't subject to as much scrutiny as business assets are, and we'll get a great interest rate because the market is tanking right now for conventional loan purchases."

Will licked his lips. "All right, I'm with you so far."

I smiled. "Then, we turn around and use that loan to fund the building of our own refinery. We can use the money from selling off our Houston headquarters for the down payment on the land, use the money from the loan to build exactly what we're looking for, and we can bypass the bullshit of this business loan altogether."

They sat silent for a pretty long time, and it made me nervous. But then, Bryce cleared his throat.

"Before I agree, I want us to crunch real-time numbers. I want us to speak with Mr. Derecho and get actual prices for the kind of land around Conroe we'd need to make something like that work."

Will nodded. "I can talk to our accountant about helping us crunch those numbers, so then we can see what kind of payment plan we're getting into and what kind of investment we can assume we'll be making."

I leaned back in my chair. "And depending on those numbers and how they shake out, we might even be able to liquidate a few things in the company that we've been talking about liquidating in order to fund any hiccups along the way so surprise monetary fixes don't sink us as badly as they would right now."

Bryce grinned. "I like this. I like this a lot. Will, when can you—?"

He held up his finger. "Hey there, Mr. Langley! I wanted to chew your ear about something for a second." Will muted himself so he could speak with our business accountant, which left Bryce and me at the brainstorming table.

"Bryce, is Luna home?" I asked.

I saw him crane his neck. "Yeah, she's in here with Willow and the kids."

"Tell her to give Mr. Derecho a call. Have her gather information on plots of land that would suit what we're trying to build and do. Then, have her call me."

He nodded. "I can do that. And in the meantime, I'm going to head over to the bank and take a peek at the renovations. I'll send pictures?"

"I'd love that, thanks. Also, are you free tomorrow for lunch?"

"I am, and I'll make sure Will is, too."

"Good. I want to shake this scenario out as quickly as possible. Because if we're going to re-file for a conventional loan, I have to catch that business loan paperwork before it goes into underwriting."

He grinned. "Should I have Mr. Derecho also look up a few houses for you to take a look at? Or, are you still considering my offer of building something on the ranch?"

I chuckled. "One step at a time. Let's get this damn refinery back home first. Then, we can talk about stuff like that."

He clapped his hands, rubbing them together. "Sounds like a plan. I'll go talk to Luna right now."

Will unmuted himself. "Our accountant said to get him the numbers as quickly as possible, and then he could have amounts for us down to the penny, depending on how much we wanted to take out as a conventional loan."

I smiled so hard that my cheeks hurt. "Great. And I'll get to work on my end with chasing down leads and halting the paperwork for that business loan."

After our video conference was said and done, I drew in a deep breath. I leaned back in my home office chair and slid my hands through my hair, feeling lighter on my feet than I had in a long time. That was how I knew I was making the right moves. That was how I knew we were finally making the right decisions. Because this no longer felt like a burden. It now felt like fun.

I'll find a way to get back to you, Luna. Even if it means selling off everything I have.

And come hell or high water, I'd make sure Luna never left my side.

Even if I had to go toe to toe with her father in order to get her.

❄ 18 ❄

Luna
One Week Later

I laid there in bed with the sun peeking through the curtains. It had been a week since Bart had left for Houston, and he was no closer to coming back. This conventional loan he and his brothers decided to execute required more upfront paperwork to fill out, and it was becoming a hassle for everyone involved.

So much so that his brothers handed over temporary power of attorney just so Bart could get through all of the signings.

My phone started ringing softly at the corner of the bed, and I rolled over. I didn't want to get up and work today; I felt too distressed. Bart should've been home by now, and with every day that passed, I expected his next phone call to be one of goodbye. The longer he stayed in Houston, the more I worried that he would end up making the choice to plant the refinery there. Or give up on this and stay with his office. Or simply not want to come back at all because he loved it there.

"Hello?" I asked groggily.

"Rise and shine, Miss Faircloth."

I giggled at the sound of Bart's voice. "Morning."

"Sleeping in because your boss isn't there to kick you in the ass?"

I rubbed at my eye. "It's only eight in the morning or so."

"Yeah, it's definitely passed ten."

I shot upright in bed. "What?"

He barked with laughter. "Just kidding. It's about eight-thirty."

I sighed. "If you were here right now, you'd pay for that."

"Trust me; I want to be there. But, hopefully, this paper-work I'm about to go sign off on is the last of it."

"Then, you'll come back?"

"That's the plan. Though, I'm prepared to stay longer if it takes longer. We need this loan to work, so I want to be here to field any issues that pop up on the same day."

I tried to hide my disappointment. "Totally under-standable."

"Has Mr. Derecho gotten back to you with those property plots? I told our accountant we'd have those to him two days ago."

I pulled my phone away from my face and checked my email. I had a message from Mr. Derecho, but when I opened it, the damn thing didn't have a bit of good news.

"Luna?"

I put the phone back to my ear. "You want the bad or the good?"

"Good, please."

"Mr. Derecho is about to hit the streets today to comb for more properties."

"Oh, boy."

I slung my legs over the edge of my bed. "But, that's also the bad news."

He groaned. "Dammit, is this thing ever going to come together?"

I stood to my feet. "This kind of thing takes time. We simply have to keep being patient."

"I know, I know. But, if Mr. Derecho can't produce something by the end of tomorrow, I'll have to find someone who can. Make sure that's communicated in your response to him."

"Noted."

I missed Bart more than I could stand, but I had no clue if the man missed me. Every time we talked, he told me about the places where he had eaten that had the best food and the bars he frequented after bank meetings that poured him the best drinks. With the way he talked about Houston, it almost sounded like he didn't miss this place at all.

Or me.

"All right," Bart said with a grunt, "I'm going to get up and get to the bank to deal with these signatures. Keep me posted throughout the day, okay?"

I wiped away at my silent tears. "Can do. Will and I are finalizing furniture prices today, and if all goes well, we will have saved the seven grand we need for the extra renovations."

"You're outstanding. And don't think I'm not trying to figure out a way to make you agree to a permanent position. Just want to make sure I've got my arguments in place first."

I snickered. "I look forward to the arguments that might not change my mind."

"Hey, I've already got you down from 'definitely' to 'might.' So, I'm taking it as a win."

I shook my head. "Have a good day, Bart."

"You too, Luna."

The second I hung up the phone, I let the tears fall. I felt more overwhelmed than I cared to admit, and the last thing I needed was to be missing some guy who didn't care about me. I put my face in my hands and let myself cry it out before I stood to head for the bathroom.

But, when I whipped my door open, I saw Will and Sadie standing there. "Oh, girl. Come here," she said. She wrapped me up in a massive hug as the decadent smells of sweet tea and cheese grits filled my nostrils.

"Thank fuck I had on clothes," I murmured.

Sadie chuckled. "I told him to wait for you in the kitchen, but he didn't listen."

I hugged Sadie tightly. "How long have you guys been here?"

She finally released me and wiped off my cheeks. "Long enough to get the picture."

I rolled my eyes. "Fantastic."

Sadie giggled. "Oh! And I have ice cream, and all of the fixings in the fridge and the freezer. Bryce and Will are taking the kids for the night so we girls can have some time to hang out."

I looked over at Will. "I really appreciate it."

He shook his head. "Not an issue at all. Plus, Sadie can't stop craving chocolate malt milkshakes. So, she's ready to have her fill tonight."

Sadie whispered loudly, "I'm going to have three of them. One for each baby and one for me."

I giggled. "You're insane; you know that?"

Will held out his arm. "Come on. Let's have some break-fast, and then we can all get to work."

The day moved at a whirlwind pace, and by the time I was done with everything on my list, the girls were staring at me as I closed my laptop.

"It's about damn time," Willow said.

Sadie handed me a bowl. "Made you this. With extra caramel and salted nuts."

I took the bowl. "Oh, hell, yes. Are we ordering pizza, too?"

Willow held up her phone. "Ten minutes out."

I sighed. "I'm so sorry that it took as long as it did. Bart just kept throwing stuff at me, and I really wanted to get it done for him before I logged off."

Sadie flopped down next to me. "Hey, I'm not judging. I'm a workaholic like that sometimes, too."

I grabbed the spoon and took a heaping bite of the ice cream, but I felt them staring me down, waiting for me to start talking. I didn't feel like doing this tonight. I was much too tired to get into the one thing the girls were waiting on me to dish about.

You need to start talking sometime. Might as well be now.

I swallowed hard. "Can I talk to you guys about—?"

Sadie exclaimed. "Yes, you can talk about Bart!"

Willow rolled her eyes. "Way to go, genius."

Sadie blushed. "Sorry."

I giggled dryly. "Is it that obvious?"

Willow nodded. "Yes."

I rolled my eyes. "Fantastic."

Sadie rubbed my knee. "Have you told him how you feel?"

I felt my eyes watering. "What? Have I told my boss that I might actually be in love with him? No, Sadie, I haven't."

Willow gasped softly. "Wait, really?"

I leaned back against the couch cushions. "With each day that passes, and he stays in Houston, I'm worried that his next phone call is going to be telling me that he's not coming back. And I really want him to come back. I want him to be there. I mean, he's the only person who makes me feel safe with everything going on right now, and it feels weird not having him here. But, I also don't want him to make the decision to stay in Conroe just for me, in case he hates it back here. You know?"

Sadie nodded. "Then, he'd resent you for coming back."

I snapped my fingers. "Bingo. You're spot on."

Willow took a big bite of ice cream. "According to Bryce, Bart hasn't enjoyed being in Houston for the better part of two years now."

I shrugged. "That's what I hear, but every time he calls me and talks about all of the restaurants and the great drinks and how nice his own bed feels, it paints a very different picture."

Sadie turned her plump body toward me. "Girl, I've seen the way he looks at you."

Willow nodded. "We both have."

Sadie sipped her milkshake. "And trust me, he's coming back for you."

I groaned. "I don't want that to be *all* he comes back for, though."

Willow shrugged. "If that's the decision he makes for himself, you don't really get a say in it."

My face fell flat. "It concerns me, so yeah, I do."

Sadie giggled. "Not this time. Where Bart wants to live and why is his business and his business alone. It doesn't concern anyone it might affect. That's the difference."

Willow paused. "You know, come to think of it? Bart has always kind of had this weird look in his eye for you."

I stood up. "I'm not going to listen to this."

Sadie pulled me back down. "It's about damn time you listened to someone. I love you, girl, but you're as stubborn as your father. So sit down and hear what we have to say for once."

I glared at her, but something in my gut told me that she was right. I'd always been stubborn and headstrong, and part of me wondered if that was playing against me right now.

Willow put down her empty bowl. "All I'm saying is this: Will and Bryce believe that Bart's always had a crush on you. But, as a boy, he was probably too scared of your dad to do anything about it."

I snickered. "Welcome to my life."

Sadie took my hand. "But, he's a grown man now. And it's very clear from the barbecue last year that he's not only not afraid of your father but very smitten with you."

I smiled softly. "You think?"

Willow giggled. "We know, you idiot."

Sadie smiled. "And we know you felt the same way about him as a kid, too."

I scoffed. "Now, there's where you're wrong."

Willow quirked an eyebrow. "So, trying to always get on the same flag football team as him in middle school was just a coincidence?"

Sadie clicked her tongue. "And making all of those jokes at his expense just to get him to look at you was all for show?"

"And constantly talking about the girls he was dating and how they were 'hoe-ish' was just you looking out for a friend?"

"And lamenting not having invitations to their popular kid parties were—"

I dropped my ice cream bowl in my lap and held up my hands. "All right, all right! Damn, I get it."

A knock came at the door, and Sadie stood. "We're just not sure how the hell you didn't see it sooner than this."

Willow cocked her body toward me. "Unless you always knew it and were too afraid to say anything."

Sadie opened the door. "Maybe because you were protecting him from your father?"

Bryce's voice sounded beyond the door frame. "Two large pepperoni, mushroom, and red pepper pizzas."

Will chuckled. "With ranch to slather on it."

I sighed. "Hi, guys."

Bryce stuck his head in. "Hey there. Also, I agree with the girls."

Will stuck his head in next. "Me, too."

I barked with laughter. "Of course, you do. You live with them."

Willow held up her hands. "Don't look at us. The theory of you protecting Bart was their idea. Not ours."

I glared at the guys. "That true?"

Bryce shoved the pizzas at Sadie. "*And*, that's our cue."

Will tossed the container of ranch dressing onto the floor, and it slid across the hardwood. "Have fun, girls. Bye!"

Willow shot up from the couch. "Here, let me help."

I abandoned my half-eaten bowl of ice cream. "I'll get plates and sweet tea for us. Unless we're doing wine?"

Sadie cleared her throat. "Yeah, sweet tea, thanks."

I giggled. "I know that, you crazy human being."

Willow stepped in front of me, blocking my way to the fridge. "And we know you need to stop worrying about what Bart might do and simply tell him how you feel."

I closed my eyes. "If he comes back to Conroe—"

Sadie interrupted me. "When, you mean."

I shot her a look. "If—and, or—when he comes back to Conroe, I'll have a talk with him. Okay?"

Willow smiled. "Pinky promise?"

I groaned. "Seriously?"

Sadie set the pizzas down. "Yep. We pinky promise, or we call Bart up and tell him ourselves."

I balked. "You wouldn't."

Sadie put her hand on the small of her back. "I'm too pregnant to be kidding. Pinky promise or we do it."

I looked over at Willow. "Fine. I pinky promise."

She smiled. "Great! Now, who's up for a movie with our pizza and ice cream."

Sadie waddled into the kitchen. "Let me make another milkshake and I'll be good to go."

19

Bart

"You're mine, Luna. You hear me?"

She moaned as my tongue fell against her clit. "Yours. I'm yours, Bart."

"Forever. No man will have you after me. Got it?"

She gripped my hair. "Ruin me, Bart. Ruin me and make me yours."

I lapped up and down her slit, committing her taste to memory as she bucked against my face. I slid a finger into her tight entrance, teasing her relentlessly as my tongue slowed its ministrations.

"No, no, no. Faster, please," she whimpered.

I teased her asshole with my finger. "More, you ask?"

She gasped. "I've never done that before."

My ears perked up. "Then, it sounds like we have a bit of stretching to do."

I felt her juices dripping down her ass crack, coating my pinky as he traced her puckered hole. I felt it opening for me. Blossoming, as if it were a wonderful little rose created for me to enjoy only. I looked up and saw her tits bouncing wildly, her pointed nipples tightening with every flick of my tongue against her swollen nub. I traced her asshole. I felt her juices coating my cheeks.

And when I pressed my pinky inside of her, I watched her beautiful body arch in response.

"Oh, fuck!"

I growled. "That's it."

"I feel so full. Bart."

"You haven't felt anything yet."

I slowly pumped my fingers as she bucked against my face. I sucked her clit between my lips, teasing her to the edge of the cliff before I ripped away from her. I rushed up her body as she begged me to keep going. I kissed up her neck, feeling her goose bumps rise against my own. I hovered over her, relishing the way she begged for me. The way she gripped tightly to my muscles. The way she whimpered and moaned only for my ears to hear.

"I need you, please," she whispered.

I kissed her lips softly before gazing into her eyes. "I love you, Luna."

And as her eyes welled with tears, I watched her lips part as if she wanted to say something.

My eyes eased themselves open, and I'd never woken up so angry in all of my life. I squeezed them shut, trying to conjure the dream as I laid there with an aching dick and a rapidly beating heart. I fisted the sheets in the palms of my hands as tightly as possible, willing my brain to recreate the euphoric sensation of almost hearing those words.

"Come on, please," I murmured. But, the dream never returned. "Fuck!" I roared.

I threw the covers off my body and stormed into the bathroom. I ran the hottest shower I could stand and washed the night sweat from my skin, only to wrap my hand around my dick and start pumping. I needed to get rid of this erection. I would never be able to think straight if I didn't blow a load against this wall really quickly. But, the only thing I thought the entire time I stroked was how it didn't feel like Luna.

"Shit," I whispered.

I leaned my head against the wall as my cock dwindled. My balls throbbed with a need for release, and I couldn't even keep my dick hard long enough to do anything about it. My head felt woozy. My stomach felt sick.

But, more than that, my heart felt empty.

Do I really love Luna?

The second I even thought about her, my heart took flight. It fluttered so quickly I thought I'd start floating, and it gave me the answer I needed. I wasn't ready to say it out loud. I wasn't even ready to imagine what it might be like to confess something like that to Luna. But, my heart already knew.

And so did my brain.

You love her, you idiot. Just say it.

"Not right now," I growled.

I reached down and flipped the water to cold, drowning out the voice in my head. I'd tackle it another day, but not right in the middle of the biggest business project my family had ever taken on. I needed to get my head back in the game. I needed to stay on top of the bank.

Like you want to stay on top of Luna.

"Come on!" I exclaimed.

I turned off the water and yanked a towel off the rack beside me. I wrapped it around me and marched out of the bathroom, running my fingers through my wet hair. I sat on the edge of my bed, wondering if a strong dose of caffeine might wake my mind up enough to stop torturing me.

Then again, the caffeine might make it worse.

When I stood to go downstairs and make some coffee, my phone started vibrating. And when I looked down, I saw Luna calling. All at once, the dream came rushing back. The sloping lines of her body and the peaks of her nipples that swelled my dick right back into place. I eased myself back down onto the bed as I reached for my phone, hoping and praying she didn't hear the sheer need for sex in my voice.

Not just sex, but sex with her.

"Shut up," I murmured.

"What was that?" Luna asked.

I shook my head. "Nothing, sorry. Just getting an early start. I see you are, too? Do you have any news for me?"

"Actually, I was really hoping to speak with you on a more personal matter."

I paused. "Oh?"

"Well, I mean, I have business to talk about as well, but I was kind of hoping I could have your ear for a second before the workday starts?"

My heart beat hard against my chest. "You can have me any way you need me. What is it?"

"*Anyway?*"

I closed my eyes. "Luna, there's actually something I'd like to speak with you about as well. Since we're on a more personal note."

"Well, you go first then. Mine kind of requires courage I haven't summoned yet."

Could it be? "Are you sure?"

She snickered. "That's the only thing I'm sure of right now."

Do it. Just tell her. "Well, I actually wanted to speak with you about what might happen once I get back into Conroe."

"So, you do have plans to come back?"

I furrowed my brow. "Why wouldn't I?"

"I don't know. You've just been in Houston for so long——"

"On business, yeah. I'm not secretly settling back here or anything."

I heard her sigh with relief. "Well, that takes a weight off my shoulders."

I grinned. "Mind if I ask why?"

I heard something tick on her end of the line before her voice sounded. "Hold on. I've got someone calling me. It might be Mr. Derecho."

"Wait, Luna. Just a second. You can call him ba——"

"I'll be right back. Don't go anywhere. Promise me."

I smiled softly. "I'm never going anywhere. I promise."

She giggled. "Good. Hold on."

I closed my eyes and forced myself to enjoy the moment. This was it. This was the moment. This was where I'd tell Luna how much I loved her, and how I want to take her out whenever I got home. I felt unstoppable, and I knew exactly how I wanted our first date to go. I remembered back to the times I had ogled her as a young man. Enjoying the way her curves surfaced and doing anything just to make her laugh. If someone really got Luna going, she snorted. And dammit, I loved that sound more than anything in this world.

So, when I heard the line click back over to my end, I drew in a deep breath before Luna's panicked voice sounded.

"I have to go. I'm so sorry."

I shot up to my feet. "What's wrong?"

"I have to go. Sick leave! I need to cash in the medical leave."

"Luna, what's happening? Who was that on the phone?"

I heard her sniffling. "The hospital, Bart. I have to go. I'm so sorry."

"Luna, wait! Who's in the hospital?"

I heard her softly crying on the other end of the line before her voice barely sounded over the phone.

"Daddy," she choked out. "Daddy's had a heart attack."

She hung up the phone, and I felt the entire world come to a screeching halt. I tried to call Luna back, but she kept shooting me to voicemail with every call that got placed through. I looked around the room, wondering what the fuck I could do that might help her from sixty miles away.

But, when my eyes landed on my suitcase, I knew exactly what I could do.

And I didn't care if it cost the family business it's fucking refinery.

20

Luna

I burst through the hospital doors. "Where is he?"

A nurse looked up at me from her desk with a deadpan expression before her eyes slid down my body. "Can I help you, ma'am?" she asked.

I strode for her apathetic presence. "Where's my father? He just came in via ambulance."

"Name?"

I blinked. "Michael Faircloth."

The woman's phone on her desk started ringing, and she turned her attention away from me. With my mismatched flip flops on the wrong feet and my hair piled into a messy bun, I felt my robe slowly slipping open. I raised up and tightened the bow around my waist as I watched this nurse have the audacity to "put me on hold," as if my father's life weren't currently hanging in the balance.

"What's your concern again?" the nurse asked.

I groaned and reached over her desk, pressing my fingers against the phone receiver until the call hung up. And when her angry eyes whipped over to mine, I leaned in close.

"Where. The fuck. Is my father?"

Her nostrils flared before she started typing away on her computer. "ICU Room 4. Now, can you move your hand?"

ICU? "Thanks. Sorry I inconvenienced your day with my dying father."

A foreign voice sounded behind me. "Miss Luna Faircloth?"

I whipped around and saw a towering man in a white coat standing behind me. "Yes?"

He held out his arm. "Follow me. I just got your father off for some testing."

I rushed over to him. "What's going on? What happened?" I didn't even care about the man's name. I just wanted to know what was going on with Daddy.

"The paramedics informed me that when he called 9-1-1, his speech was slurred. He was complaining of pain in his upper back and the base of his skull, and by the time he got here, his pupils were force-dilated."

Tears brewed behind my eyes. "Do you know what's wrong with him? Why is he in ICU?"

We took a hard left at the end of the hallway before the

doctor started walking faster. And I didn't like the hastiness of his words that matched his movements.

"He's in ICU because I have an idea of what's happened to him, but I need tests to back up my theory," he said.

I gripped his arm and stopped us in the middle of the hallway. "Tell me your theory."

He sighed. "If I'm wrong, I'm going to worry you for nothing."

I glared up at him. "I'd rather have half-answers than nothing at all. Tell me what you're thinking."

He slid out of my grip and pointed down another hallway before we started walking again. "I'm pretty sure your father's had a stroke."

My heart plummeted to my toes. "A-a-a-a... a stroke? How bad?"

"That, I won't know until the tests come back. But, his speech was already slurred, and he was having issues with movements in his left arm and leg. I'm almost positive that's what's happening."

I swallowed hard. "Happening. As in...?"

The doctor stopped in front of a room. "As in, it's still currently happening."

Tears slipped down my cheeks. "What do we do? What happens from here?"

He leaned against the wall. "We take it minute by minute. If the clot's small enough, there's a chance that a small dose of radiation will break it up and allow it to pass naturally."

"And if not?"

He shrugged. "Anything from surgery to blood thinners for the rest of his life to physical therapy in order to regain movement again."

"Does this have anything to do with his hip replacements?"

The doctor blinked. "What?"

"His hip replacements. My father had both of his hips replaced last year. He's been struggling through physical therapy—"

"Exactly how long ago were these replacements."

I shook my head. "Nine, ten months ago? Just shy of a year."

"And he's still in physical therapy?"

I nodded. "And on regular pain medication. But, his surgeon said that would be normal, given my father's medical history."

He pushed himself off the wall. "I need you to give me all that you know about your father's medical history. Because this changes a lot."

I rattled off as much as I could, but I knew there was still stuff I was leaving out. I talked with him about my father's tolerance for pain, and how sometimes he wouldn't even know that he was sick or injured until it got to a worsened state. I recounted my father's open-heart surgery when he had a bypass a decade ago because of a heart attack that came out of nowhere. The doctor jotted down everything I said before ushering me into the ICU and running off. And as I paced the room, waiting for Dad to come back, I had this sinking feeling in the pit of my gut.

What if this is it?

When I wore my legs out, pacing the floor of his hospital room, I slouched into a chair in the corner. Time seemed to move like molasses being poured out of an ice-cold jug, and all I wanted was to have my father back. Whatever condition he was in, I'd take care of him even if it meant finally moving out of my apartment and moving back in with him for good. I'd happily be his caretaker. Count his pills and wash him down at night. I'd do whatever it took to help keep the man who raised me and loved me unconditionally as comfortable as possible.

Then, almost three hours later, his hospital door burst open. "Ah, you must be Luna," a soothing female voice said.

I didn't pay attention to it, though. All I could watch was my unconscious father being rolled into the room. The nurses maneuvered him into the corner by the window before they started fiddling with his tubes—IVs in each hand, tubes up his nose, a catheter protruding from between his legs that fed into a bag with urine that was darker yellow than anything else.

And his face—I couldn't get over how pale his face had become.

"Dad," I whispered.

"Forgive my rudeness when you first came in. My name is Doctor Weatherford."

I mindlessly shook the man's hand as I stared down at my father. "Do you have the results of his tests?"

He clasped his hands behind his back. "A few of them, yes. His potassium levels are through the roof, which is why he was experiencing the pain in his chest and at the base of his skull. We'll be flushing his system throughout the night to get them back down to within a normal range."

I finally looked up at him. "What about the imaging tests? Did he have a stroke?"

"I don't have them back for you to see, but I watched the results as they happened. Yes, your father's had a stroke. But, he's lucky."

Relief washed over me. "Why?"

The doctor looked back over at my father. "His physical therapy kept his blood pumping, and it managed to dislodge some of the clot that was building up. But, his clot is directly related to his hip replacements. He's allergic to the material they've used for the implants."

My jaw dropped open. "What?"

"It's uncommon, but it happens. The surgeon should have performed an allergy test before the surgery, so I'm pulling those records to check to see that the test happened. If it did? I'll try my best to backtrack why the test didn't show anything."

"And if they didn't do the test?"

The doctor shrugged. "I can't tell you what to do with that information. But, either way, it's good information to have, don't you think?"

The idea that my father's surgical team of nurses had fucked up that badly made me sick with anger. I slowly walked to his bedside and pulled up a chair, reaching for his frail hand. I'd never seen my father's skin so pale. I'd never felt him so cold in all my life.

He looked so small and fragile, nothing like the man that raised me.

"I'm here, Dad," I whispered.

And even though he didn't open his eyes, he squeezed my hand.

"Daddy," I breathed.

The doctor walked up beside me. "He's very weak. He might not be asleep, but it'll be a couple of days before he's even got the strength to open his eyes. And as soon as we can, we're going to be getting him back into surgery with our best replacement surgeon to switch out those implants."

A tear streaked my cheek. "He'll have to start all over with his physical therapy."

"Which is why I'm going to leave you some information about in-home care. Your dad's got a long recovery ahead of him, and the two of you are going to need help."

I could've sworn I saw my father's lips downturn at the mere mention of 'help.'

"I appreciate it, Doctor Weatherford. Thank you so much."

He patted my shoulder. "The next twenty-four hours are critical. But, if we have no hiccups between now and then, we can move him to a regular room."

I looked up at the doctor. "He feels so cold. Is there anything we can do about that?"

He nodded. "I'll see about getting him a heated blanket."

"I appreciate it, thank you."

As the doctor vacated the room, I stood up and smoothed my father's wispy hair back. As I gazed down into his face, trying hard not to cry against his skin, fear washed over me. This was straight from my nightmares—the worst-case scenario brought to life. I sat down and threaded my fingers with my father's hand, allowing my cheek to rest against his hospital bed.

"We'll do this just like we always do," I whispered through my tears.

I need to put in my sixty days at my apartment complex.

So many things started rushing through my mind. I'd have to quit my job working for Bart so I could go back to taking care of my father. I'd have to prepare my childhood bedroom to be lived in, which meant removing the twin-size bed in there to make room for the queen-size bed I now owned. I'd have to get the girls to help me move my clothes and stuff.

I'd also have to shelve my personal life again.

Why is it always us?

Every time it seemed like my life was finally getting back on track, something had to come around and take me out at the knees. I felt selfish for being so upset while my father's half-dead body was there in an ICU bed, but I couldn't help myself. All my life, I'd been dedicated to helping others, assisting them in their time of need, and sparing them from the negative. Whether it was turning down boys I liked just so they wouldn't have to meet my father, or whether it was comforting my father in his time of sadness when my mother had died.

It always seemed to be "world first, Luna second." And I couldn't see straight through my tears anymore.

How did everything go so wrong so quickly?

All I wanted was a decent shot at life like my best friends. All I wanted was one chance to carve out a life for myself that wasn't dependent on the well-being of others around me. All I wanted was one shred of beauty in my life that wasn't there for any other reason other than my own damn happiness.

But, as I sat there with my father's almost-lifeless hand in mine, I stuffed down the selfish feelings. I stuffed down the emotions. I stuffed down the tears and the pain and the inevitable issues I'd have to face.

And I turned my attention to what I could do to help my father in any way possible.

❧ 21 ❧

Bart

I burst through the hospital doors. "Where are they?" I heard a nurse sigh heavily from the front desk, and I strode up to her.

"Name, please?" she asked.

I planted my hands onto the fake wood of the desk. "Michael and Luna Faircloth. What room are they in?"

The apathetic nurse started typing away at her computer before her phone started ringing. And when she reached for it, I picked up the phone and dropped it back into the receiver.

"Room number. Now," I commanded.

She scoffed. "I see the two of you are alike."

I blinked. "Excuse me?"

The woman pointed. "ICU, Room 4. Doctor Weatherford is the assigned physician on duty right now."

I nodded. "Thank you for your help."

"You and everyone else," she murmured.

I brushed off the need to fire back at her and slammed through the metal double doors. I followed the navy-blue and white signs pointing me toward the ICU block, and when I got to the end of the hallway, I took a sharp turn to my left. I broke out into a jog, following the burnt orange lines as I weaved my way through the corridors of the hospital.

And after getting turned around twice, I found myself in front of ICU Room 4.

"Can I help you?" a voice asked.

I turned around and found myself eye to eye with a man in a white coat.

"Dr. Weatherford?" I asked.

He nodded toward the door. "Are you here to see Mr. Faircloth?"

I nodded. "And support his daughter, Luna."

"She's a strong woman. She's been by her father's side since she got here."

I turned to face the door. "How bad is it? Do you know what happened?"

"Are you family or next of kin?"

"I might as well be. All of us are very close. We're all Mr. Faircloth and Luna have some days."

The doctor eyed me carefully before he caved. Almost as if he didn't feel like fighting anymore.

Guess Luna's been riding him pretty hard.

The doctor sighed. "I got his test results back about an hour ago. Mr. Faircloth has had a clot-related stroke because of an allergic reaction he's having to his hip implants."

I furrowed my brow. "He had those replacements, like, a year ago."

"Yes, but it's not uncommon. According to the medical history Miss Faircloth gave me, between his high tolerance for pain and his disdain for doctors, it doesn't shock me that he's been battling this for so long. It's why we highly recommend in-home help as opposed to familial help. There are tests an in-home nurse could have performed that would have caught this reaction before we got to this point."

I puffed out my cheeks with my sigh. "Am I allowed to go in?"

"Normally, we only allow one person in the room with the patient at a time. But, as long as you stay out of the way of nurses, I'll allow it this one time."

I patted his shoulder. "I appreciate it."

"Do something for me, though."

"Anything."

The man leveled his eyes with me. "Luna is already speaking of helping her father in any way she can. Try to communicate to her how imperative it is that an actual, medically-trained professional take care of him. I don't have the heart to tell her that the lack of medically-trained individuals present is what got her father into this mess."

I reached for the doorknob. "I know exactly how to do

that. Thank you, Doctor."

He patted my shoulder. "Press the red button on his bed if you need anything. But, come seven-thirty, you're going to need to find your place in a waiting room. Dr. Shropshire isn't as forgiving of visitors as I am."

"Noted. And thank you. Again."

The doctor walked away, and I slowly inched the door open. I tried to move as silently as possible, especially considering the fact that I heard soft snores already coming from the room. I slipped inside and cracked open the door just in case anyone needed to get in. And as I silently walked over to a hunched-over Luna with her cheek against the hospital bed mattress, I pulled up a chair to sit beside her.

Her head whipped up. "Doctor?" she asked groggily.

I chuckled. "Never had a passion for getting an MD."

She slowly looked over at me. "Bart?"

I smiled softly. "How are you holding up?"

Almost as if the action answered my question, she flung herself into my arms. I held her closely, scooping her into my arms and placing her in my lap. I felt her sobbing against the crook of my neck as I wrapped my arms around her, trying to blanket her from the cruel, harsh world that seemed to keep beating her and her father down.

"*Shh*, sh sh sh sh. It's okay. I'm here now," I whispered.

She spoke through her sobs. "He's—had a—a-a-a..."

I kissed her forehead. "I know. I spoke with the doctor outside."

She started coughing. "Why are you—you here?"

I snickered. "Do you really have to ask?"

And when she looked up at me with her red, watering eyes, I felt my heart tug in my chest.

"Bart, I—"

I let my forehead fall against hers, and it silenced her words. "I'd never leave you alone during something like this. Ever. I just hate that it took me even this long to get back."

She straddled me, and it made my heart skip a beat. "I'm so glad you're here. Thank you for coming."

I nuzzled her head until her eyes locked with mine. "We're going to get through this, okay? But, we're going to do it the right way this time."

She furrowed her brow. "The right way?"

My eyes danced between hers. "We can talk about that later. But, just know that the right way doesn't always involve family doing everything."

She blinked. "I can't let some stranger—"

I pressed a finger to her lips. "It's got nothing to do with strangers and everything to do with medical professionals. Your father needs the care of someone who's medically trained. That's the point he's hit. You can help, but you can't do everything he needs. And there's nothing wrong with that."

Tears flooded her cheeks. "He's not going to like that."

I cupped her wet cheek. "Well, he's a big boy. He can deal."

She giggled and wiped at her tears, sniffling to try to keep her composure. And this time, I was the one who couldn't help myself. With my heart taking flight and her body heat radiating around me, I leaned forward and planted my lips against hers, feeling her kiss back as the saltiness of her tears spread along my tongue.

I slid my hands into her arms as she draped her arms around my neck. Dammit, I'd missed this woman, and it felt wonderful to have her back in my arms, even with the circumstances at hand. Our tongues collided in a soft dance as our lips undulated together, carving out the smallest piece of paradise in what seemed to be the middle of hell.

And when we finally came up for air, I found Luna smiling at me.

"There she is," I whispered.

She giggled softly. "I'm really glad you're here."

"So am I."

She settled her cheek against my shoulder, and a few minutes later, her soft snores joined her father's. Nurses filtered in and out every hour, on the hour, and all of them seemed to completely overlook my presence. I unraveled her hair from its messy bun and stroked my fingers through it. I slowly worked out all of the knots and kinks before pulling it back into a low ponytail so it didn't continue to pull at the top of her head. Mom had always dealt with migraines because of how tightly she kept her hair pulled back, and the last thing Luna needed to deal with was something like that.

Then, a knock came at the door.

"Who is it?" Luna asked as she ripped her head up.

I chuckled as the door eased itself open, revealing Dr.

Weatherford. "May I have a second with you, Miss Faircloth?"

Her eyes grew worried. "Is something wrong?"

"No, no, just wish to speak with you in private."

She looked back at me. "Bart can't come?"

I looked over at the doctor before he sighed. "I'm going to need you to amend and sign off on a HIPAA statement before you leave, okay?"

Luna slid down from my lap. "That's fine. Bart?"

I stood to my feet. "Lead the way, Doctor."

We left Mr. Faircloth's side before another team of nurses slipped in, probably to draw blood and run some more tests. I felt Luna slip her hand into mine, threading our fingers together as we walked behind the doctor. I looked down at our connection before a smile spread across my cheeks. And the tighter she clung to me, the more powerful I felt.

I'll help get you and your father through this. Whatever it takes.

"Step into my office," Dr. Weatherford said.

Luna and I slipped in before he followed us. And when he closed the door, I felt Luna flinch.

"Is everything okay?" she asked.

The doctor nodded. "Just wanted to get away from everyone filtering in. Our mornings are busier than most people expect, and I wanted some privacy for this conversation."

My stomach seized. "What's going on?"

The doctor looked at me. "While the nurses are checking Michael's potassium levels, I want to speak with the two of you about your rights regarding negligent medical care."

I blinked. "Why the hell would we need something like that? And what's wrong with his potassium levels?

Luna patted my chest with her free hand. "Dad came in with high levels of potassium in his system, which attributed to the back and neck pain he was feeling."

I looked down at her. "And the negligent medical care?"

She looked up at me with her big puppy dog eyes. "I'll let Dr. Weatherford explain."

So, I turned my attention back to him. "What's going on?"

The doctor sighed. "Normally, in the medical community, we try to help save our colleagues from things like malpractice lawsuits and the like. They have a nasty tendency to ruin entire careers, and we try our best to make sure that never happens."

But...?" I asked.

"But, before every replacement surgery, an allergy test is supposed to be run. It's a very simple test: a nurse draws blood, and the lab runs tests on it with the implant material to make sure the sample doesn't react."

Luna swallowed hard. "They didn't do that test, did they?"

The doctor shook his head. "I've placed a call to the head of his surgical nursing team to see if the results were misplaced, and I haven't told them my thoughts or feelings on the matter. It's not my place. But, when the surgical hospital finally sent over his medical records, the test results—or any indication that the test had been performed—weren't there."

Luna's lower lip quivered. "That facility has almost killed my father."

I squeezed her hand. "We don't know that yet, though. They could've just not added the test results to the main file. It happens sometimes."

Dr. Weatherford nodded. "And it's what I'm trying to figure out. But, if I can't find those test results, I'm going to have our hospital lawyer meet with you personally. I can't engage you on what you should do, but I can inform you and direct you toward multiple sources of other information that *can* get involved and help you."

I felt my blood boiling. "Thank you, Doctor. That's very kind of you."

Luna sniffled. "Yes. It's very generous. I can't thank you enough."

He looked at his watch. "All right, it's time for me to get home so I can see the kids off to school. Dr. Shropshire should already be clocked in, so just remember that only one of you can be in the ICU room at a time."

I nodded. "We appreciate everything you've done tonight."

The doctor opened his office door. "I wish you the best of luck with everything. I'll update Dr. Shropshire myself on what's going on so he's completely on top of what I already know."

And as the doctor led us back to Mr. Faircloth's room, my mind started spinning with all sorts of things.

Namely, if this kind of thing were something our family attorney could get involved with.

✵ 22 ✵

Luna

The hours seemed to pass by quickly and slowly at the same time. Dr. Shropshire hadn't come by, and it was already lunchtime. We hadn't heard anything about that allergy test, which made me even more nervous. I mean, even if a doctor had been negligent, it wasn't as if we had the money to do anything about it.

My father was on a fixed income. I made good money working with Bart, but I hadn't been working with him for long. I had a whopping three-fourths of a paycheck in my bank account and almost nothing in my savings. One more good hard knock from life and it was over for the both of us.

"What am I going to do?" I whispered.

Bart started massaging my shoulders. "I don't want you to

worry about that right now. Let's get your father home first, and then we can go from there."

I tilted my head back and looked up at him. "They'll have to replace both of his hips again. He'll be right back at ground zero."

He dipped down, kissing my forehead. "And we'll take it one step at a time if that's what has to happen."

The door to my father's room opened, and a nurse shuffled quickly inside. I watched as she picked up my father's arm and stuck him with a needle, drawing a vial of blood as if we weren't there.

"Nurse?" Bart asked.

"Yes?" she asked, not looking up.

"Are there any updates on his condition?"

A booming voice sounded from the doorway. "I believe I can answer that question."

I stood to my feet. "You must be Dr. Shropshire."

He walked over and stuck out his hand. "Miss Faircloth. Mr. Remington. I'm sorry we're meeting under these circumstances."

Bart and I shook his hand before I drew in a deep breath. "What's going on?"

"Got it," the nurse said.

The doctor nodded. "Get it tested ASAP. I want a rush on it."

Bart wrapped his arm around my waist. "Why the rush?"

Dr. Shropshire clasped his hands behind his back. "My colleague, Dr. Weatherford, filled me in on what's going on with your father. I've been on top of researching some alternative solutions to the issue at hand."

I folded my arms across my chest. "Why? Because a colleague of yours might be in trouble?"

He chuckled. "Many people paint me to be a hardass, but I can assure you I'm simply thorough. Plus, the hospital did find those test results."

I blinked. "They did?"

He nodded. "They did. They performed two of them, actually, because the first material your father *was* allergic to."

"H—he was?"

He nodded. "Yes. But, the second test they performed, his results were just fine. I had them send me over the surgical footage since your father had his hips replaced in a training hospital, just to make sure they used the right implants for the surgery."

"And?" Bart asked.

"And they did. So, we've ruled out the idea of an allergic reaction."

I sighed. "Hence the research you've been doing."

The doctor handed me a file. "Does any of this look familiar to you?"

I took the folder from him. "What is it?"

"Just open it up and take a look at the pictures. I want to know if any of these things are around your house at all."

I furrowed my brow. "Uh, okay. Yeah, sure. Hold on."

I opened the folder and flipped through the pictures and recognized a lot of the items mostly because they were basic things found in most homes in the US—enriched white flour, full-sugar sodas, bananas, regular vitamins.

I shook my head. "I don't get it. What do these random things have to do with my father?"

"How many of those items do you think are in your house that your father consumes regularly."

Bart interjected. "Can we skip over the dramatics and get to the point where you tell us what's going on?"

The doctor slowly looked over at him. "All right. Here's what I believe: Mr. Faircloth is currently allergic to his own blood."

I blinked. "I'm sorry, what? I thought Dr. Weatherford said my father had a stroke?"

The doctor looked back down at me. "Oh, he did. But, the underlying cause of that stroke and everything that's been cascading before that has a different underlying reason. He's allergic to his own blood right now. That's why I had my nurse draw some because a simple antibody identification test will tell me if my theory is correct."

I shook my head in disbelief. "How's that possible? And, what does that have to do with the sodas my father drinks?"

The doctor perched against my father's hospital bed. "It's called Autoimmune Hemolytic Anemia, and it happens whenever a person's immune system triggers a bodily response to destroy its own red blood cells. Sometimes, the trigger can be as simple as stress, but sometimes it can be triggered when foreign objects are introduced into the body."

Bart clicked his tongue. "Like the hip replacements."

Dr. Shropshire drew in a deep breath. "Exactly. And that wouldn't have registered on any allergy test at all. The response would've started with a bit of joint pain, which could have easily been attributed to just going through major surgery. Add the concoction of pain pills on top of the bananas your father was probably eating by the pound because they probably made him feel better, and we've got a compounding issue that's nothing more than a dull roar until the liver can no longer filter out the nonexistent toxin."

I paused. "The broken red blood cells?"

The doctor nodded. "Essentially."

Bart held me tightly against his side. "What do the bananas have to do with anything, though?"

The doctor set down the chart at the foot of the bed. "Potassium has a plethora of benefits. It regulates fluid levels, which is why doctors recommend regular potassium intake after most surgeries. It also helps reduce blood pressure problems, which I see your father has in his chart. But, the biggest benefit, in some cases, is the fact that higher amounts of potassium help regulate heart rhythms. Great for those who have had bypass surgeries, like your father. But, when coupled with something that's attacking red blood cells, all that does is shoot those pseudo-toxins through the body faster."

"Jesus," I breathed.

Bart sighed. "So, what do we do? Where do we go from here?"

The doctor slid his hands into his pockets. "The good news is that your father probably won't have to have his implants replaced. If the surgery is what triggered this response, then putting him back under is only going to make it worse. What I'm going to do is have the head of our dialysis department come in after her lunch break and speak with you about getting him set-up with in-home dialysis treatments. Filtering out those attacked red blood cells with dialysis is going to help his body regain some of its strength and function, and he is going to be able to level out. The reason why his immune system is doing this is that it's much too taxed, and it can't figure out why so it's producing antibodies because it thinks its sick. We have to filter that stuff out and give his body time to recuperate from being in constant overdrive, and with some close in-home monitoring, we should be able to get his body back in functioning order by the end of the year."

My eyebrows rose. "That quickly?"

A nurse rushed in with a piece of paper and handed it off to the doctor before slipping back out the door. And when Dr. Shropshire slid it into my father's file, a grin crossed his face.

Dr. Shropshire smiled. "That quickly. And now that I've got confirmation of the antibodies present in his blood, I can schedule your appointment with the head of our dialysis department."

Before I could think, I threw myself at the doctor. I felt so relieved and so overjoyed with this hopeful news that I didn't even think twice. The doctor chuckled as he patted me on the back, then I felt Bart slowly prying me from around the man's neck. And when I wrapped my arms around Bart, I started crying tears of relief and happiness against his chest.

"Thank you so much," I said through my tears.

Dr. Shropshire chuckled. "It's my pleasure. This is what I live for: helping families get answers. But, if the two of you are going to be in here together, the door needs to stay open. Okay?"

Bart started rubbing my back. "Of course. And thank you for everything."

I heard my father groaning and shifting around in bed, and it caused me to dart back to his side. I took his hand in mine and held it up to my lips, kissing his knuckles as his eyes slowly opened. He tried to shift himself around, and I reached over, pulling and tugging until he was on his side.

And when his tired eyes found mine, I leaned down and kissed his cheek.

"It's so good to see you awake," I whispered.

Bart chuckled. "Welcome back, Mr. Faircloth. You really gave us all a scare."

My father's eyes danced between mine before he looked up at Bart. "So, you're the boy my daughter's been living with."

And his words brought the entire room to a grinding halt.

23

Bart

I knew the man wasn't stupid. I knew he would've heard about that by now. Conroe was small, and anyone who thought they could hide anything in this town needed a reality check. I'd never tell Luna that, of course. But it was the truth.

And as panic washed over her features, I simply nodded.

"Yes, sir. That would be me," I said.

Luna scoffed. "How in the world did you know?"

Mr. Faircloth chuckled. "Sweetheart, I love you. But it's a small town. Everyone here knows everything. My neighbor told me about a week ago what was going on."

I sat on the edge of the hospital bed. The one thing I knew about Luna's father was the fact that he was an intimidating man. But, even the most intimidating of men had morals and rules by which they lived their lives.

And I knew once he understood the situation, he'd be okay.

"Sir, I want to start by apologizing. I should've come to you when the decision was made. But, Luna and I figured it was better in our current circumstance to keep things as under wraps as possible."

His eyes slowly panned up to mine. "What circumstance?"

Luna's voice grew worried. "Daddy, please take a breath. You're in an ICU room. You don't need to be getting riled up."

His voice fell into a gruff tone. "I'm not riled, anything. I just want answers."

I nodded. "And I would, too. Did Luna tell you her apartment was broken into?"

She hissed at me, "Bart, stop. Let me handle this."

Her father held up his hand, silencing her words. And while I didn't like that, I loved Luna. So, I'd always do what was best for her. Even if she didn't agree with me at the moment, I'd always make sure every action I took was to the benefit of her future.

Holy shit, I love Luna.

"You gonna talk, son?" Mr. Faircloth asked.

I licked my lips. "We haven't heard from the police since the start of the investigation about three or so weeks ago, but Luna's apartment was broken into. The place was trashed. And given the fact that the police thought it might've been because of a man who's known to terrorize women around the area, we all came to the conclusion that Luna didn't need to be staying at her place until the police could check things out. But, we also didn't think it was smart for her to go back to living with you in case it wasn't just a random coincidence of some sort."

Her father nodded, but he sure as hell didn't say anything.

"Daddy?"

He didn't acknowledge his daughter. "So, how the hell did you two end up living together?"

I shrugged. "Simple. Willow and Bryce offered for Luna to stay in their guesthouse, and I offered to stay in one of the guest bedrooms out there so she didn't have to stay alone. She admitted to me that she was still pretty wary of being by herself, so I packed a bag and fixed the problem."

"Uh-huh."

I nodded. "Simple as that."

He quirked an eyebrow. "A different room, you say?"

I held up my hands. "I'd never disrespect your daughter— or you—that way. Luna deserves better than that."

I saw Luna out of the corner of my eye hanging on to our every word as Mr. Faircloth's eyes slowly slipped down my body. He could study me all he wanted to, though. I had nothing to hide. There was nothing wrong with our truth, and if he got mad about it, then that would be a personal problem he could deal with on his own.

After all, each of us was a grown adult.

I knew this was the first step to getting in his good graces, though. I'd heard the stories of how many boys Luna had turned away in high school because of her father. And I wouldn't be another notch on that particular post. I loved Luna. I wanted to take care of her. Protect her. Provide for her, especially since I had more than the means to do it. And I knew that for any loving father who cared for his daughter, that was enough.

At least, it should be enough.

"Dad?" Luna asked.

He looked over at her. "Is he telling me the truth?"

I buried my smile as Luna nodded. "Yes, he is."

"Your apartment was actually broken into?"

She took his hand. "Yes, it was."

His voice grew pained. "And you didn't tell me? You didn't think that was something I should've known?"

She sniffled. "You're already going through so much, and I didn't want to worry you."

"You know damn good and well it's not your job to—"

"Of course, it's my job!" she exclaimed.

She shot to her feet, and my eyes widened. "This asinine idea you have about me not worrying about you is bullshit, Dad! You're my father—my daddy. The man who raised me and protected me, even when I didn't agree with it. You gave up everything for me, especially after Mom died. Why in the world wouldn't I worry about you like you worry about me?"

The room fell silent at her plea, and I watched Mr. Faircloth carefully.

"She has a point," I said.

He shot me a look. "I'm aware of that."

I grinned as Luna sat back down, taking his hand. "I'm sorry for raising my voice, but I'm not sorry for what I said. All my life, you've been nothing but stubborn to a fault. You've been overprotective, bull-headed, and downright insufferable some days. But that's what makes me love you. Your fierce need to protect me is one of the many things I love about you. And I knew it might actually kill you if I told you something like that happened and you had no way to keep me safe."

They stared at one another for a long time before his eyes came back to me.

"What are your intentions with my daughter?" he asked.

Luna paused. "What?"

I smiled. "They're simple, Mr. Faircloth: I want to love and take care of your daughter the way you always have."

Luna squealed, "*What?*"

Her father nodded. "How many women have you fallen in love with in your life?"

Luna scoffed. "Can we please not act like I'm not here?"

I peeked over at her. "Give us a second, beautiful, okay?"

She balked, but she did as I asked. And it made her father chuckle.

"Never seen anyone do that to her," he murmured.

I settled my hand on his shin. "I've been in love with three women: my high school girlfriend, which lasted a whopping four months; an assistant in my geologist office back in Houston, which I never acted on because she apparently didn't like men."

Her father barked with laughter as I turned my eyes to Luna. "And the third?" he asked.

I winked. "Your daughter, sir. Timetable, to be determined."

Her eyes watered. "You—you love me?"

I nodded. "I do, Luna. I realized it when I was in Houston. I missed you, and I missed having coffee with you, and I missed working side by side, and I missed the fire that rushes through your veins. The zest you have for life."

Her father cleared his throat, and my attention turned back his way.

"I'm serious, Mr. Faircloth. I'm in love with your daughter. And I'll do whatever it takes to keep her happy, protected, and never wanting."

He nodded slowly. "How's the petroleum business going?"

I shrugged. "Hitting a couple of financial snags with this refinery, but we're picking up the slack."

"What kind of snags?"

"Daddy, I don't think this—"

He cut Luna off. "What kind of snags, Bart?"

I snickered. "The kind that come with having to take out a personal loan to do business instead of a business loan to do business."

He furrowed his brow. "Not enough physical collateral to offset the loan?"

I blinked. "Yes, actually. How did you know?"

He shrugged. "That's usually the issue that happens with businesses. I encountered it myself when I was younger."

Luna clicked her tongue. "What in the world are you talking about?"

He looked over at his daughter. "You aren't the only one with secrets. I just know how to keep mine better."

"What? Daddy, you're not making any sense."

His stoic eyes turned back to me. "Your honesty is refreshing, Bart. I'll give you that. Do you have plans to marry my daughter one day?"

Luna groaned. "You know that's up to me, Dad."

I chuckled. "I do have plans to at least ask one day, yes."

She whipped her head over to me. "You do?"

Mr. Faircloth nodded. "You know what you have to do then, right?"

I smiled. "Yes, I do. You okay if I do it now?"

"I really hate this," Luna murmured.

I snorted. "No, you really don't."

She rolled her eyes, but again, she didn't protest. And it made her father smirk. But, it didn't deter me from my path.

"Mr. Faircloth—"

"Michael, please."

I nodded. "Michael, I'd like to officially ask for your permission to, one day, ask your daughter to marry me."

"I think I'm the one having a stroke now," Luna said breathlessly.

Her father barked with laughter. "You know, I could tell at that cookout that the two of you had something going on.

The way you looked at each other and whatnot. It's how I used to look at her mother."

"Daddy," she whispered.

He took her hand, but his gaze didn't waver from my face. "What I want for my daughter is to have the kind of life her mother and I had. A life where she's always got a partner who will fight for her heart every day he gets up. A partner who will raise her up when she's down, but a partner who will also respect her independence and never force her to get rid of that just because that's what he thinks a woman should do."

I patted his shin. "You have my word—that's my absolute intention with Luna one day."

"Then, when you're ready, you have my permission."

I looked over at Luna and saw her eyes bursting with more tears. Only this time, they were tears of joy instead of sadness. I stood from the bed and held out my hand for her, watching her slip her delicate fingers into my palm. I raised her up to her feet before I reached into my back pocket, feeling that damned piece of jewelry burning a hole in my ass.

"What are you doing?" Luna asked.

Her father snickered. "I know what he's doing."

Then, I got down onto one knee as I held the sparkling diamond ring up for her to see.

"Are you kidding me right now?" Luna asked.

I smiled so hard my eyes closed. "I love you with everything I am, Luna. And I think in some ways, I've loved you from afar for a long time. Ever since we were children, I thought you were wonderful—strong and intelligent. You had this love and respect for your family that rivaled my own, and it only made you more beautiful in my eyes. And when I was in Houston, I passed by this jewelry shop that had the most incredible engagement ring, and I thought to myself, 'one day I'm going to give Luna a ring just like that.'"

A tear slid down her neck. "You did?"

I nodded. "The thought came so clearly to me, and it felt so right to me that I couldn't pass up the opportunity. There are people in this world who date for years before they're ready to make that commitment, and then there are people who just know. I know with you, Luna. Even if you don't know it yet—even if you can't say 'yes' yet—I want you to know that I know. And when you're ready, like I am, this ring will be here for you."

She wiped her tears away from her face. "Ask me."

I paused. "Really?"

She nodded. "Ask me, Bart."

I stood to my feet and cradled her left hand in my palm. "Luna Faircloth, will you make me the happiest man on this planet and be my wife?"

She giggled with tears in her eyes as she looked up at me. "I love you, Bart."

My heart warmed with ecstasy. "I love you, too."

"And yes, it would be an honor to be your wife."

24

Luna

After almost a week of being in the hospital, we were discharged with new prescription medications, standing dialysis appointments, and information on how to schedule regular in-home nursing care for my father. The idea of someone else taking care of him still didn't sit right with me. But, Bart helped to convince me that just because I thought my father deserved family around didn't mean I had to be the one taking on all of his care, especially with a wedding to plan.

"I still can't believe it fits," I whispered.

Bart chuckled. "I kind of had to eyeball your ring size from my memories, but I think I got it all right."

I looked over at him. "All right? This is more than 'all right.' This is perfect."

"I'm glad you like it. I saw it in that shop window and thought of you instantly."

My father piped up from the back seat. "Save the kissing until I'm inside, yeah?"

I giggled. "Whatever you wish, Dad."

"Can I make a suggestion for the wedding, though?"

I craned my neck back. "Of course."

"No destination weddings, please. I'd like to actually be there when you get married."

I snickered. "Be there? Old man, you're walking me down the aisle, even if you have to use crutches to do it."

"Hey, who you callin' old?"

Bart eased us into my father's driveway. "We're home! And perfect timing, too. It would've been a shame for my fiancée to be killed by her father before we can even start planning this wedding."

We all started laughing as we piled out, and Bart was kind enough to help my father into the house. I rushed around with his new medications under my arm, trying to pick things up and toss trash into the half-open trash can. Already, I saw how my father had been living since I'd moved into the guest-house. The trash on the floor and the still half-damp towels scattered about. My father needed some serious help.

I sighed. "Bart, maybe if I just move in for a few—?"

My father's voice fell hard against my ears. "Luna, look at me."

My eyes gravitated to him. "Yeah, Dad?"

He broke away from Bart and hobbled in my direction. Where he then took my cheeks in his hands and brought my face close. "I love you with all my heart. But you have to stay out of my house."

I blinked. "What?"

His hands fell to my shoulders. "There are things I like that I can't do with you around."

I scoffed. "Like what!?"

"Like, sit around naked on my couch and have a beer while watching *Jeopardy* without being judged for it."

I wrinkled my nose. "Do you know how many times I've sat on that couch?"

"And you don't even want to know how much I enjoy sitting on my back porch with nothing but a towel wrapped—"

I held up my hands. "Okay! Placing calls to the in-home care office now!"

Bart and my father broke out in laughter as I made my way into the kitchen. I had no idea if my father was being serious or silly, but I wasn't willing to move back in just to figure it out. And he had a point. My father was a grown man with his own ways, even if he was a bit immobile at the moment. Just like he would've been impeding on my personal space if the tables were turned, I was impeding on his.

And I felt a weight finally lift from my shoulders.

I sat at the kitchen table and called down the list of numbers until I came to a home care agency that was taking new clients. I jotted down payment information and the cost of part-time versus full-time versus twenty-four-seven in-home care. I wasn't sure if my father would like the last option, but I wanted to know all of my options if push came to shove.

"Hey, Luna?"

I turned my head toward Bart's voice and covered the receiver of my cell phone. "What's up?"

"Do you have that vitamin list in your bag? I figured I'd run out to get those."

I smiled. "Yeah, my purse is on the counter. It's a pink sheet of paper."

"You sure you want me to go through it?"

"You have my permission this one time, okay?"

He nodded. "You want anything while I'm out?"

I pointed at him. "We need more milk in the guesthouse. And cereal. I think we've eaten through all of it."

He pulled out the pink slip of paper from my purse. "Noted. I'll pick up something for us to eat, too. We can have dinner with your father before we head back."

I blew him a kiss. "You're the best, thank you so much."

He winked. "Not as 'best' as you, but I'll take it."

The front desk woman finally made it back to our phone call, and I scheduled an appointment for a nurse to come out and evaluate my father. His evaluation would determine the kind of care the office was equipped to dealing with, and the entire time I couldn't stop staring at my ring. The girls would never believe it. I mean, engaged? Already!

And yet, it somehow felt so right.

Righter than anything I've ever done before.

After making the appointment with the care office, I started to clean. Dad had already fallen asleep on the couch, so I took advantage of the silence. I picked up the trail of half-wet towels and tossed them into the washer. I walked into my father's room and turned my nose up at a stench that I distinctly attributed to his socks lying in the corner. With my breath held and my gut steeled and strong, I picked every-thing up off the floors and tossed them in with some heavy-duty laundry detergent. Then, after the washer started up, I walked into my father's bathroom.

"One more clean-down won't hurt," I murmured.

I scrubbed away at his tub and his toilet. I mopped the floor and wiped down the mirror before organizing things around his sink. I made my way into his bedroom and fluffed his pillow, even going so far as to strip the sheets from his bed to remake it.

But, when I went to reach for the duster in his closet, I felt a hand on my shoulder.

"It's time to head out, Luna," Bart said.

I gripped the duster. "I just need to get these cobwebs and—"

He placed his hand on my forearm. "There aren't any cobwebs."

I looked over at him. "I mean, sometimes we can't see them, you know?"

He sighed as he slid the duster out of my hand. "Your

father is going to be just fine. I've already hired a maid service to come in once a week and take care of this kind of stuff. Between that and the in-home—"

"You did what?"

He tossed the duster into the closet and placed his hands on my shoulders. "I picked up the vitamins he needed and put them in the half-bath downstairs. And while I was out, I contacted Maria."

"Who's Maria?"

"She's Bryce and Willow's maid. She's been a wonderful help for them for the past three years or so she's been there. Her daughter is following in her footsteps, so to speak, and was looking for some work. So, I hired her daughter to come by once a week and do everything you're doing right now."

I blinked. "You—you did?"

He led me toward the door. "Yes, I did. I knew it was something you'd worry about, so I took the liberty of getting ahead of the problem. Between his in-home care and Maria's daughter's help, it'll be like you're here, except you won't have to actually be here."

I sighed. "You're incredible; you know that?"

He kissed the top of my head. "As are you. It's one of the many reasons why I love you and why I want to marry you. But, you have to learn to draw boundaries with people, even with your own family."

"I know. I know I do."

He held my hand as we walked down the stairs. "And I'll

help you do it. Just know that, sometimes, the best thing a family can do is back off."

Dad sat up on the couch. "He's got that right."

"Dad," I said breathlessly. I rushed to his side, but he held up his hand and shot me a look.

"This right here is what he's talking about," Dad said as he propped himself up.

I rolled my eyes. "I'll work on it, okay? But, it won't get better overnight. It'll take time."

He nodded. "I know it will."

Bart walked up to us in the living room. "Need a pillow?"

Dad nodded. "And a glass of water. But, have Luna get it. I want to talk with you a bit more."

Bart sat down on the other side of the couch. "Of course."

I kissed Dad's forehead. "Be right back."

As I slipped a pillow behind his back, I went to get some ice water from the kitchen. But, when I crept back down the hallway, I heard the two men I loved most in my life talking lowly among themselves.

And I couldn't help but eavesdrop.

"You boys still going to be reckless and do that personal loan?" Dad asked.

Bart sighed. "Honestly? I don't even think that's going to work. Even if we got the personal loan to go through, there's still a matter of selling off our old headquarters to fund hefty renovations. It's essentially a crapshoot. With the personal loan, we've got one shot and zero room for fuck-ups."

I furrowed my brow as Dad nodded, as if he understood what Bart was saying.

How does he get it?

"Well," Dad said, "if you boys went back to the business loan, how much would you still need to front to make it work?"

Bart snickered. "At least a million. Though it would be closer to two in order to make all of us more comfortable."

"You got any more room for investors?"

What the hell?

Bart blinked. "Yeah, we've always got room for that."

Dad nodded. "What do your investors buy at in?"

"Uh, our newest investor bought in a valuation from three years ago, so I'd probably give someone a fair shake and continue with that valuation."

"Which is?"

Bart paused. "Eight hundred thousand for four percent."

Dad didn't even hesitate. "Make it ten for the two million and you've got a deal."

I couldn't contain my reaction. "*What?*" I leaped from around the corner and sloshed cold water all over my hand.

"What the hell just happened?" I asked breathlessly.

Bart looked up at me. "I'm honestly not sure myself."

Dad chuckled. "I'm sure he'd have to get approval from his brothers, but I'm pretty sure I'm investing in my new son-in-law's business."

I set the water down on the couch-side table. "You don't

have two million dollars, Dad. This isn't some sort of a—a loan or something you can pay in installments."

He blinked. "Yeah. I know."

I paused. "You're on a fixed income!"

"I know that, too."

I threw my hands in the air. "Can someone please explain to me why we're struggling to make ends meet, but somehow my dad's got two million lying around in a couch somewhere?"

Dad shrugged. "I mean, not a couch, but..."

I glared down at him. "Spit it out, Dad."

He waved his hand in the air. "Money needs to be grown, Luna, not shown. I made some good investment deals when I was younger, even though your mother about killed me some months."

Bart finally spoke. "If someone knows their way around the stock market, then theoretically—"

My eyes bulged. "Does anyone find this as ridiculous as I do?"

Dad smiled. "Your mother did."

I swallowed back a growl. "No wonder people in town call you a cheapskate."

He shrugged. "A badge I wear with pride. If I weren't one, I wouldn't be able to help right now, would I?"

I shook my head. "I just always thought you were a rancher, Daddy. A rodeo competitor in the summers. Stuff like that."

"And I was, sweetheart. But, I'm also other things."

I drew in a sobering breath. "We've got a lot to talk about

once you have the strength to take my verbal lashings. You know that, right?"

He smiled lovingly up at me, and it made my heart melt. "Whatever you need."

I sighed before I bent over and kissed his forehead, and then I looked over at Bart, who was still sitting there with shock in his eyes and his jaw swinging. It made me giggle as I reached over and closed his mouth with my fingertips, shocking him back to life before he drew in a quick breath of air.

"Like you said, I'll have to talk to my brothers, but I'm sure they won't have an issue with it at all," he said.

Dad nodded. "Good. Get my number from Luna, and just let me know how you want the money delivered."

"Wire transfer will probably be easiest."

He held out his hand. "Then, it's settled."

And when my fiancé and my father shook hands, it forever redefined for me what a "family business" looked like. It solidified a future I'd always been trying to carve out for myself, and it made my heart swell with happiness. I found a man my father saw as an equal. I found a man I could respect and love and devote myself to without losing my independence and what made me, well, *me*. In some crazy whirlwind of events I still couldn't sort through, my life had been plunged into darkness before being ripped into a light so bright it threatened to blind me for the rest of my life.

And it was a fate I'd happily accept if this was the outcome.

A family—rooted in business and in love—who stuck by one another through thick and thin.

It doesn't get any better than this.

Then, my phone rang.

"Hello?" I asked.

"Miss Faircloth?"

I furrowed my brow. "Who is this?"

The man cleared his throat. "Officer Rinkinson."

I rushed into the nearest corner. "Hey! Hi! Uh, wow, I wasn't sure if I'd hear back from you guys. How are—well, how are things?"

He snickered. "They're better as of an hour ago."

I blinked. "Why?"

And when the police officer assigned to my case uttered those perfect words, I realized that all things could get better given time. "We got him, Luna. We caught the son of a bitch."

EPILOGUE

Bart
One Year Later

I looked in the mirror as my best man—my father— straightened my bow tie. I drew in a deep breath as Bryce brought my white suit jacket over and slid it up my arms. And when Dad smiled at me, Will yelled from the bathroom.

"You got that red rose to pin on your titty yet?"

I rolled my eyes. "If you call it 'titty' one more time, I'm gonna punch you."

Dad chuckled. "And a bloody nose isn't a good look for a wedding."

Bryce snickered. "I'll kill you if you get blood on this jacket. It was made specifically for your body, and it's expensive to get these things dry-cleaned on a rush."

Will jogged up with the rose. "That's why you should've gotten two jackets."

I smiled. "Just pin the damn rose on me."

Will smirked. "On your what?"

I lunged at him playfully, and we all fell apart in laughter. I hooked my arm around Will's neck, and he quickly tapped out since it was easy for my fingers to reach his tie. Dad pulled us apart before taking the rose from Will, and he calmly pinned it against the left side of my chest.

Directly over my heart—on my lapel.

"Thanks, Dad."

He dusted off my shoulders. "This is a proud moment for your mother and me. You boys have come so far."

"Don't make me cry. I didn't sign up for that part."

He cupped my cheek. "You'll do plenty of that once you see Luna in her wedding dress. She looks breathtaking."

My eyebrows rose. "Really? You've seen her?"

He nodded. "Your mother sent me a picture and made me promise not to show it to you. But, yes. I've seen her. And I can't wait for you to see her, too."

Bryce patted my back. "You did good with that one."

Will walked around and stood beside Dad in front of me. "I knew they'd eventually find one another. It was only a matter of time."

I rolled my eyes. "Yeah, yeah, yeah. You know everything. I get it."

Will nodded. "Now, you're getting it."

I shot him a glare just as Uncle Ryan walked in and offered his congratulations too. Then Dad gathered us all up for a round of pictures. A photographer had been following us around all day, but I wanted some pictures that weren't simply candid. However, just as we gathered, I felt my phone in my pocket vibrating. And as Dad shot me a nasty look, I dug it out of my pocket.

Please let this be the phone call.

"Hello?" I asked as I answered, my heart hammering in my chest.

"Mr. Remington. It's Officer Rinkinson."

I snickered. "No need to be so formal, Andy. But, please tell me you have good news."

He chuckled. "Sorry to bother you on the big day, but I wanted to call you right as court let out."

"And?"

I held my breath as I heard cars honking on Andy's end of the line.

"Two years for the stalking and harassment, and two more years for the break-in, robbery, and vandalism. Plus, probation for a year on an ankle monitor once he gets out because of priors he only served a short sentence for."

I breathed a sigh of relief. "I can't wait to tell Luna. Thank you so much, Andy."

"We've been waiting to put this guy away for a while. We've been watching him escalate for some time, and I'm glad we've finally gotten him off the streets."

I held a thumbs up to Dad, and everyone started silently

cheering around me. It felt like a ten-ton weight had been lifted off my shoulders. After that asshat had been caught trying to flee the state in his rickety camper-van, he'd been arrested and processed before having his bail revoked for being a flight risk. And even though it took a while to get the guy in court, we finally did it.

We rid Luna of that bastard forever.

"I really appreciate this, Andy. Everything you and your team did for us," I said.

I heard his smile through the phone. "Happy wedding day, Bart. Now, go get your girl."

I hung up the phone and turned toward the photographer to catch some candid photos just before I took my vows. And the smile plastered across my face was one for the books. We snapped a few funny ones before I hugged Dad and my brothers, trying to capture the magic of this day from beginning to end.

And after snapping a few photos to be added to the ever-growing reel, I drew in a deep breath.

"Since we're all here," I said.

Dad groaned. "Here we go."

Bryce snickered. "And everyone calls me the workaholic."

I held up my hands. "Nothing like that, nothing like that. I just wanted to ask Dad if he's popped by the refinery yet."

Dad slid his hands into his pockets. "Actually, I did. It's looking really nice, too."

Bryce nodded. "We had some hiccups there with the remodeling of the main building. But, the plumbing was more intact than what we thought, so it didn't cost us as much as we were originally quoted."

Will licked his lips. "And with this being the last of the renovations, the refinery will go through its first test run while Bart here is on his honeymoon."

I pointed at him. "You better keep me updated, too. I want to know if there are any snags."

A knock came at the door before it eased open, and I saw my mother's smiling face. She looked like the picturesque version of pride today, and the beautiful red ensemble she donned really made her eyes sparkle. Every time Dad looked her way, we saw the love he had for her. It was the same kind of love I felt whenever I looked at Luna, and it was the same kind of love Bryce and Will had whenever they looked at Willow and Sadie.

How we all got so lucky, I'd never know. But, I'd also die in order to protect it.

"We're ready when you guys are," Mom said.

I smiled. "We'll head out there now."

Her eyes watered. "My boys look so grown up."

Dad chuckled. "Let me get her out of here before she cries all her makeup off."

She scoffed. "I have more control than that. I gave birth to three massive sons without medication. I'm pretty sure I can make it through a wedding."

Dad peered over his shoulder and mouthed, "ten bucks, she cries," and the three of us nodded.

I'd totally take him up on that bet.

As the three of us made our way up to the front of the church, I gazed out at the sea of faces that had come to celebrate this incredibly special day with all of us. There had to be at least five hundred people packing this place out, but it would be worth every penny. This was a day none of us would forget. It was a day we'd look back on with nothing but smiles on our faces and joy in our souls, especially since things with the refinery were finally where they needed to be.

When the minister joined us at the front of the church, the procession music started. The string quartet played a beautiful piece I didn't recognize as my father and the rest of the groomsmen moved slowly down the aisle, with Mom already having to blink away tears as she stood on Luna's side of the stage.

Well, not *just* Luna's side.

"Here she comes," Will whispered.

Willow was the first to appear, being escorted down the aisle by her father. She held her head high in her gorgeous champagne-colored dress that clung to her body and trumpeted out into a gigantic train that took two people in back just to keep it straight. It was dramatic and sparkly. It made her look like a princess. And when I looked over at Bryce, I saw him wiping tears away from his eyes.

Then, Will stepped to the forefront.

Up the aisle came Sadie, with her head held high, as her strapless princess gown flared out so much at her waist it almost took up the entire aisle on either side of her. She had on a dress she always touted as "eggshell," which was apparently different from champagne. According to the girls, at least. She had a big bow nestled in the crook of her waist, accenting the subtleties of her body that I saw Will ogling.

And when she finally got up to the stage, I saw Will's eyes misting over, too.

Then, as my heart pounded in my chest, I exchanged places with my brother. With the two of them standing behind me, all time and sound seemed to cease as the doors opened. The first person I saw was Michael, clad in a tuxedo that made him look a thousand times stronger and more intimidating than ever. But, when Luna emerged in her wedding gown, a knot formed in my throat.

My God, she really is breathtaking.

She had a crown of white roses nestled in the big curls of her hair that fell down just past her shoulders. Her spaghetti-strapped dress hung daintily against her, framing her curves in a way that made me salivate. I swallowed hard, trying to keep my cool as her hips swayed side to side. Ruffling the fabric and making it undulate as if the energy of the ocean waves fueled the beauty of her dress.

And when Michael escorted her to me, handing her over for me to take as my wife, a tear slid down my cheek.

"You leave me speechless; you know that?" I whispered.

Her dazzling brown eyes gazed up at me as she smiled. "I really like this coat on you. I hope you bought it."

I nodded. "I'll make sure to wear it often."

The wedding itself moved in a blur. I couldn't take my eyes off Luna, and I damn near forgot the vows I had written because I couldn't stop staring at her. I stumbled my way through them, feeling like a damned idiot. But, when I finally got to the end of them, I got to slip that ring on her finger and bring her against me in a deep, luscious, passionate kiss.

While the crowd that had come to celebrate with all of us stood to their feet and clapped.

Luna and I stepped first off the stage, and I scooped her into my arms. She squealed with delight and kissed me one last time as people threw crimson red rose petals into the air. With Bryce and Will behind me, scooping their women into their arms, I carried the love of my life down the aisle. Feeling her tongue tangle with mine as silky rose petals graced the floor beneath us.

Signaling the start of our lives together.

The photographer wrangled our large family out front for some pre-reception pictures as the limo pulled up. Maria stepped out with the kids, and we waved her into the photos, proclaiming that she was just as much a part of this family as the rest of us were. We jumped in the air and took silly face pictures with the kids. We did pictures with just the women and just the men before breaking off into family units and doing our own little photo shoot.

Then, after the photographer was satisfied, the three happy couples piled into the limo. So we could make our way to the reception hall.

"Holy shit," Willow said breathlessly.

Sadie giggled. "Took the words right out of my mouth."

Bryce leaned forward. "Maria told me she's going to take

the twins home. They're getting a bit antsy, so she wants to get both of the little guys fed and down for a nap."

Worry crossed Sadie's face. "Are you sure she doesn't need my help?"

Will took her hand and kissed it. "I promise, our boys are going to be just fine. They're in great hands."

I nodded. "Plus, Maria's got her daughter helping out today as well. So, she's not alone."

Sadie sighed. "Oh, yes that's right. Thanks for reminding me."

It tickled me to know that they named their baby boys after Will and Dan, after Dad, especially when Sadie had been so adamantly against it, at first. But, sometimes, when you know something, you just know, and not everyone can always explain it. For some people, it's naming their children. For others, it's finding their life partner.

And as I slid my arm around Luna, I relished the fact that I had found my person. The woman who had been made just for me.

"So, are you going to update us?" Sadie asked.

Luna cleared her throat. "Huh?"

Will chuckled. "Already worn out from today?"

Luna sighed. "It's been a whirlwind, that's for sure."

Willow leaned forward. "She couldn't sleep last night from all of the excitement."

I peered down at her. "Is that true?"

She looked up at me. "Let's just say I'm going to need a lot of caffeine to finish out today?"

I grinned. "Whatever you want, that's what you'll get."

"Hello!" Bryce playfully yelled, "we'd all like an update on the house, please!"

Luna giggled. "Can't you just look out your back window and see it for yourself?"

I laughed. "I didn't purchase a plot of land *that* close to my brothers. We need at least a shred of privacy."

Will smirked. "And I know what for."

I shot him a look. "You don't get to make jokes about my wife like that now, okay?"

Luna patted my chest. "Ah, my fierce protector."

Willow giggled. "Guess women do sometimes marry men like their fathers."

Luna rolled her eyes. "Anyway, the house is coming along great. All they have to do is finish up the guest bathroom and paint the outside. Everything else is finished."

Bryce popped open a bottle of champagne. "That, in and of itself, calls for a celebration. Because it's hell in a hand-basket building a house anywhere, much less a two-story home with a wrap-around porch."

Will reached for a crystal flute. "And don't forget those columns. Those things alone are a pain in the ass."

Sadie scooted closer to me. "Did you end up putting the lake in front of the house or behind the house?"

I smiled. "Why don't you come over after we get back from our honeymoon and see for yourself?"

Will leaned into the conversation. "Uh, because we honeymoon after you guys do. So, she'll come to see it when we get back just before her cousin Ellie comes for a visit."

Willow raised her hand. "Oh, did you just mention Ellie is coming to visit you guys?"

"Yep, she's thinking about moving here when..."

"She's still single, right?" Willow butted in.

"Yes, yes she is."

Willow grinned, "Well, then, we will have to make sure to introduce her to *Uncle* Ryan."

Luna giggled, "There she goes again... the queen of matchmaking."

Before Willow could defend herself, Sadie turned her eyes out the window. "Who the hell is that?"

We all looked out the windows before Bryce groaned. Will told the girls to stay in the limo as it pulled right up to the reception hall, and I had half a mind to tell these reporters to fuck off. Sure, they were from *Forbes Magazine*, but this was our wedding day.

A quote could happen after we enjoyed ourselves.

Still, my brothers and I slipped out of the limo and walked right up to the woman with the recording device. She asked us a few questions about our "vintage bank" headquarters that had been up and running in Conroe for the better part of the last eight months. We talked about the employees we already hired and the jobs we were looking to hire for in the future. Will quickly went over the design elements Luna helped him with, and Bryce rattled off some numbers on how much our conferences would bring, monetarily, to our small hometown.

Then, the reporter for the magazine asked us a question that caught us off-guard.

"How do you boys feel about your parents moving back home? Will they be building on the infamous Rocking R Ranch property like the three of you have?"

I blinked. "I'm sorry, what did you say?"

Dad made his way down the stairs and interjected himself into the interview. "And this is where *Forbes Magazine* needs to excuse themselves since they've already spoiled our surprise."

The reporter blushed a deep red before turning off the recording device.

"I'm so sorry. I figured they already knew," the reporter said.

Bryce looked at our father. "Is it true? Are you and Mom moving home?"

Dad patted mine and Will's back. "Well, with the grand-kids you guys are pumping out for us, we figured there's a lot of spoiling to be done. So, yes. Your mother and I are in the process of moving back home. We should be settled in by the time all of this honeymooning is done."

My brothers and I sent up cheers of happiness before we embraced our father, showering him with kisses. We heard the limo door open as the girls slipped out, wiggling their way into the party. We could tell they were confused, but they rejoiced with us anyway. And as I wrapped my arms around Luna, I picked her up to swing her around before her beautiful red lips crashed against mine.

"I love you," she whispered.

I placed her back down onto her feet before my hands settled into the small of her back. "I love you, too," I murmured.

She smiled. "What's got you guys so happy?"

I nuzzled her nose with my own. "Mom and Dad are moving back to Conroe."

Her eyes widened. "What? That's great news! When?"

Dad chuckled behind us. "Come on. Let's get you guys into the reception and get to dancing. We can talk about logistics later."

And as I threaded my fingers with Luna's, all of us proceeded into the reception hall. Walking beside our wives, smiling from ear to ear, and silently rejoicing that our lives had finally gotten on track. No matter how quickly—or how slowly—things happened.

Nothing could get better than this.

Follow Ellie and Ryan story in
Cowboy's Tempting Neighbor

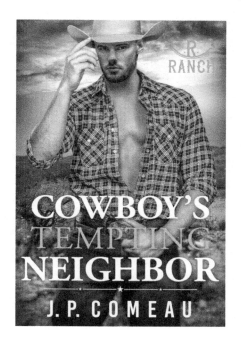